*To my darling Flanna,
I leave you love and more.
Within thirty-three days of your
thirty-third birthday you will have a legacy
of which your dreams are made.
Act selflessly in another's behalf,
and my legacy will be yours.
Your loving grandmother,
Moira*

Too bad Flanna McKenna didn't believe in the spirit of the legacy. Oh, she believed in the powers her grandmother left her. It was the promise of love that left her cold inside.

Or did it?

Was there another reason Michael Eagan had found her on her thirty-third birthday...?

PATRICIA ROSEMOOR

IN NAME ONLY?

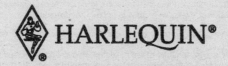

TORONTO • NEW YORK • LONDON
AMSTERDAM • PARIS • SYDNEY • HAMBURG
STOCKHOLM • ATHENS • TOKYO • MILAN • MADRID
PRAGUE • WARSAW • BUDAPEST • AUCKLAND

As always, thanks to my critique group—Sherrill, Cheryl,
    Rosemary and Jude—and to Rebecca/Ruth for their
continuing support. And to Marc for the pawnshop idea.

ISBN-13: 978-0-373-69314-6
ISBN-10:   0-373-69314-1

IN NAME ONLY?

ABOUT THE AUTHOR

Patricia Rosemoor has always had a fascination with dangerous love. She loves bringing a mix of thrills and chills and romance to Harlequin Intrigue readers. She's won a Golden Heart Award from Romance Writers of America and Reviewers Choice and Career Achievement awards from *Romantic Times BOOKreviews*, and she teaches Writing Popular Fiction and Suspense-Thriller Writing in the Fiction Writing Department of Columbia College Chicago. Check out her Web site: www.PatriciaRosemoor.com. You can contact Patricia either via e-mail at Patricia@PatriciaRosemoor.com, or through the publisher at Patricia Rosemoor, c/o Harlequin Books, 233 Broadway, New York, NY 10279.

Books by Patricia Rosemoor

HARLEQUIN INTRIGUE
707—VIP PROTECTOR*
745—THE BOYS IN BLUE
    "Zachary"
785—VELVET ROPES*
791—ON THE LIST*
858—GHOST HORSE
881—RED CARPET CHRISTMAS*
924—SLATER HOUSE
958—TRIGGERED RESPONSE
1031—WOLF MOON**
1047—IN NAME ONLY?**

*Club Undercover
**The McKenna Legacy

CAST OF CHARACTERS

Flanna McKenna—The Irish psychic saw only death and destruction in the pieces of the cursed Celtic collection that she replicated for the murder victim.

Michael Eagan—The no-nonsense, tough P.I. began by investigating a murder in Boston, then followed the trail of theft and murders to Ireland.

Bridget Rafferty—The murder victim made the mistake of wearing the cursed jewelry.

Barry Rafferty—Why is the older son so frantic to get his hands on the valuable collection?

Katie Rafferty—Why wasn't Bridget's mother with her as planned on the night of the murder?

Eamon Rafferty—Did the younger son's need for money put him in cahoots with a convicted thief he considered a friend?

Hugh Nolan—The houseman seems to know everything going on at Rafferty Manor.

Lisa Madden—Bridget's grieving friend had her own suspicions about who did it and why.

Sean Hogan—The convicted thief says he had nothing to do with the crimes.

Joseph Begley—Did The Traveller really not know the identity of the man who'd hired him?

Prologue

County Clare, Eire

The mists off the Shannon estuary rose around the towers and turrets of Rafferty Manor, wreathing them with a wet silver cloak, perfect cover for the thief to get inside without being seen by prying eyes. The house itself was dark. The lady of the manor had announced her intentions of visiting her daughter in Dublin for the week and had given most of her staff time off. The few remaining at the manor were undoubtedly asleep.

Luckily, no break-in was necessary. A key from under a cement cherub opened the side door near the car park. And the code to disable the alarm was a simple one—Bridget Rafferty's birthday.

The stone-and-wood hallway was dark but for a single low light near the side stairs, which were carpeted to assure silence. The master suite—or should it be called the mistress suite since a widow alone occupied it?—lay to the back of the house.

The suite itself consisted of two oversized rooms and an equally imposing marble bath. The bedroom's furnishings, including a four-poster, were of rich cherrywood. The sitting room had a fireplace with hand-carved wood and imported tiles, plus windows with a view of the magnificent gardens.

An uninformed person would look for a wall safe or perhaps a larger safe in the walk-in closet, but in reality, the silly woman was so trusting she left her most valued possessions in plain sight. Or nearly. The dressing table held a secret drawer, one that popped at the touch of a hidden switch.

All one had to know was where.

One did.

The drawer swished open and there they lay—a reminder of their Celtic heritage. Pieces of jewelry from a collection of Celtic design commissioned during the Middle Ages. Not crafted of gold and having neither diamonds nor precious stones in the settings, the pendant and earrings had been of poured bronze and silver, the threads twined into spirals and knots and decorated with cabochons of fire opal. And yet this collection was worth more than others…and more than mere money.

But wait! Where were the other pieces? The bracelets and ring and headpiece?

Frustration seethed through the thief as the necklace slipped easily into a velvet pouch. The McKenna woman! She had agreed to replicate the collection. She must have the other pieces!

Suddenly the room blazed with enough light to make a heart stop.

"What are you doing in my quarters?" The lady of the manor stalked forward, her expression confused until her gaze dropped to the drawer. "I—I don't understand."

"You weren't supposed to be here!"

Her eyes and mouth widening in shock as understanding dawned, Bridget said, "Plans change."

Tragic for her. Only one solution to this problem existed. It wasn't supposed to be this way, this time. But it seemed violence was inevitable.

"I can't believe you would steal from me!" Bridget shouted.

Unwilling to suffer the consequences of being caught red-handed, and needing to act fast before a scream brought the remaining servants running, the thief picked up a heavy candlestick from the dressing table and swung.

Chapter One

"May the road rise to meet you. May the wind be always at your back," Father Seamus O'Reilly intoned over the coffin in the small graveyard behind St. Mary's Church.

Flanna McKenna stood with the other mourners in the drizzle as fine as a fairy's breath. Used to the weather that kept the land green, most didn't bother to protect themselves.

"May the sun shine warm upon your face. And rains fall soft upon your fields."

A soft day appropriate for a burial, Flanna thought. Bridget Rafferty had been a grand woman with a generous spirit. The crowd around her grave proved how many people she'd touched. In addition to her children—Barry, Eamon and Katie—the wealthy stood among Bridget's servants and people of every class in between. It seemed the whole town of Killarra had turned out to bid her one last goodbye.

"And until we meet again, may God hold you in the hollow of his hand," the priest said, finishing the traditional Irish blessing.

Such a shame—such a crime—that Bridget's life had ended so tragically.

But hadn't that been the curse of the Celtic jewelry collection, the reason the older woman had wanted the pieces copied in the first place? Flanna thought, watching mourners file past the coffin, which would be lowered after they all left. As Flanna had already informed the authorities, Bridget had planned on keeping the copies and donating the originals to the Irish Museum.

Flanna gazed around at her fellow mourners, wondering if the murderer was among them.

Surely not.

"Oh, dear Bridget, may you be in Heaven a half hour before the Devil knows you're dead," Lisa Madden said, choking back a sob.

Apparently the women had been good friends despite the difference in age—Bridget more than sixty, while Lisa looked to be on the light side of forty, with shoulder-length blue-black hair and unlined fair skin. Lisa had gone through a box of tissues between the viewing and the funeral mass and the grave site, and her carefully applied eye makeup now pooled below her gray eyes.

Flanna couldn't help but offer comfort. "A cuppa, perhaps?" she asked, thinking tea would soothe her.

A pat on the woman's back served to jolt Flanna into taking a step away. She felt bereft as it was and didn't need the Madden woman's strong emotions adding to that burden.

"A whiskey would be more to the point," Lisa said, wiping away her tears as she moved away from the grave site.

Then the distraught woman straightened her spine and rose to her full height. Much taller than Flanna, who was five-four, she had a regal quality to her, emphasized by a tailored gray suit that nevertheless allowed her to look feminine.

"Sure and this never should have happened," Lisa said, stopping for one glance back at the coffin.

"Right you are, and I know you'll be missing her."

"If only the darling woman had stayed in Dublin with Katie instead of returning early…"

Flanna suspected timing wouldn't have mattered. Bridget had not only acquired the pieces, but had also made the mistake of wearing them. The dead woman had activated the curse… Flanna kept that thought to herself. Whenever she spoke of out-of-the-ordinary circumstances, she saw how people looked at her—either with amusement or as though they thought her daft.

She certainly wouldn't reveal what she'd learned through her own gift.

"If only she had listened to me," Lisa mourned, adding a final sniffle.

"About what?"

"She never should have bought Caillech's treasures. I tried to talk her out of it."

"You believe in the curse, then?"

"I'm Gaelic through and through, Flanna McKenna. Of course I believe! They say Caillech herself lives in the cabochons and takes revenge on anyone who wears what is hers."

Knowing this, Flanna nodded but kept from adding that legend also said that Caillech would be able to free herself and return to corporeal form—the form of the wearer but with the power of the sorceress—if the whole suite was brought together and worn by the new owner on Beltane, the anniversary of Caillech's death. Not that Bridget had purchased every piece. There was still a girdle belt and brooch missing. Thankfully, for Beltane was but a week away.

"I'll be thanking the both of you to keep from soiling my mother's good name with such nonsense."

Flanna whirled to see Bridget's red-headed offspring in a phalanx behind her. Young Katie was weeping, Eamon glowering, and Barry, the one who'd spoken, had his nose ever-so-slightly in the air.

"I meant no disrespect to your mother," Flanna said. "But the curse is no secret."

"I told Mother not to involve a McKenna," Barry said, shaking his head. He was a big man with a wide girth and jowly face, and his posture disclosed his self-importance. "A weird lot, all of you McKennas. But Mother wouldn't listen to me. If she had—"

"She might be alive today," the younger and slighter Eamon finished for his brother.

"You don't think *I* had anything to do with her murder?"

Barry's expression, set in stone, told her he did. "You'll be handing over the pieces of the collection still in your possession."

Not liking his tone or the accusation, Flanna said, "When you pay me for my work. A cashier's check will do."

She feared that he might write a personal check and then cancel it before she could get it to the bank. She'd rented a cottage here in Killarra just to do the work for Bridget, and she still had to pay for her flat in Dublin. Her finances were sorely depleted.

"I do have a contract," she went on, "and I was to be paid in full on receipt of the final pieces, which I have completed. You'll get both the originals and the copies when I get my compensation."

Barry looked ready to choke. "I won't be able to manage that until Monday—"

"Then Monday it will be."

"In the meantime, the *gardai* will be checking on you, sure enough," Eamon said.

Flanna couldn't believe the younger, slighter-of-build brother was now threatening her with a visit from the authorities.

She'd done nothing wrong!

"Perhaps the only pay you'll be owed is three meals behind bars," Barry said, his voice tart with satisfaction.

Eamon added, "If you had anything to do with our mother's death, you'll certainly not go free."

The fragile-looking Katie suddenly spoke up. "Stop it, both of you! Put the blame where it belongs. It's my fault she's dead!"

The brothers acquiesced, and Barry pressed his siblings to move off to the car park and their waiting Mercedes.

"Her fault?" Flanna murmured.

"Katie and Bridget had some terrible fight. I don't know about what, but it's the reason Bridget came home early. That must be why Katie blames herself. If her mother hadn't left Dublin when she did…"

"She would be alive today." Feeling badly for the young woman, Flanna said, "Thank goodness her brothers don't blame her."

"Don't let them get to you," Lisa said softly. "Grief makes one mad."

Their grief riled Flanna inside, but outwardly she kept her temper. "Bridget believed, too, you know. A pity she was tempted into wearing Caillech's treasures."

Nodding, Lisa asked, "Shall I save you a seat at lunch, then?"

When Flanna shook her head—she was too upset to eat—the other woman moved off. The crowd had thinned out, mourners no doubt heading for Garrity's pub, where a buffet lunch was to be served. The drizzle had stopped and the few raised umbrellas were lowering.

That's when she saw the stranger on the far side of the grave. The way he was looking at her put a knot in her stomach and a tickle in her throat. She noted every detail about him despite the distance between them. With hair that shone blue-black and eyes that gleamed nearly as deeply blue as the Irish Sea, he was a fine-looking man who filled out the shoulders of his navy suit jacket quite nicely.

A man she had never before seen.

So why was he staring at her as if he were trying to see inside her?

Instinct made her move away fast. Flanna's pulse threaded unevenly, and her breath caught in her throat. She didn't glance back, just walked as fast as she could to the car park. It wasn't until she was opening the door of her car and getting inside that she looked up to find that the stranger was following her. She ignored his wave imploring her to wait so he could speak with her, and started the engine.

Not wanting to speak to someone she didn't know, Flanna drove off, heading not for her own home but for the small town where her parents lived. Irony of ironies, today was her birthday, her thirty-third, and Ma and Da were making way too much of a fuss, insisting on throwing a family party and all.

What a way to start the celebration—with a funeral.

Turning onto the national road that would take her to Lough Danaan in Co. Cork, Flanna glanced in the rearview mirror and caught a glimpse of a dark blue Renault doing the same. Probably one of Bridget's rich friends.

Her thoughts turned to the kind and generous woman. Flanna would mourn her. Bridget had known about the curse on the jewelry. That was the reason she'd hired Flanna to make the replicas in the first place. But the doomed woman hadn't been able to resist wearing the real thing in the meantime…just that once.

Obviously, once had been enough.

Sunk in gloomy thoughts of death and destruction, Flanna was halfway to her parents' house before realizing the blue Renault was still right behind her. Surely it wasn't following her, she thought, her fingers tightening on the steering wheel. The road was a double carriageway, with vehicles passing at will. But not the Renault, not even when she slowed to see if the driver would become impatient. Kilometer after kilometer, it stayed directly behind her, the same several car lengths back no matter what speed she took.

Was she really being followed?

Unable to get the thought out of her head, Flanna felt herself react to the situation. Her stomach twisted into a knot and her pulse sped up. The turnoff to Lough Danaan couldn't come too soon for her.

One small part of her thought that surely the Renault would keep going on the larger road, but no, it turned and stayed directly behind her.

What to do?

There would be people at her parents' home, including her second cousins Aidan, Cashel and Tiernan McKenna, three of the biggest, baddest lads a lass in need of protection could wish for. The thought settled her down even as she wondered what the man following her wanted.

Only one way to find out.

Parking behind several other cars in front of her parents' home—a two-story limestone building with extensive gardens that had been lovingly planted by her Grandmother Moira— Flanna steeled herself as the Renault pulled in right behind her. She exited the car and stood fast, ready to scream for help if necessary. The man exiting the Renault was the same man from the grave site.

The one who'd been staring after her.

"Flanna McKenna, wait a moment."

Pulse thudding, she stopped, drew herself to her full height and demanded, "And what is it you would be wanting?"

"To talk. About your work for Bridget Rafferty."

"Unless you represent the authorities, which I doubt with that accent—" he was obviously an American "—I have nothing to say to you." How would a complete stranger from another land know about her work?

"Michael Eagan, Beacon Hill Investigations." He pulled out a leather wallet and flipped open his identification. "It seems your Mrs. Rafferty was the third murder connected to the theft of antique Celtic jewelry in the last month, the first having been in Boston."

"The third?" Flanna's mind whirled. "Of course, the other pieces…"

"So you *do* know something about the murders."

The way he said it put up Flanna's back. Another person who thought she was guilty of something? Though she wanted in the worst way to tell him to leave, she couldn't do it just yet, not until she got the details. She'd not only experienced bad vibes from the pieces she'd replicated, but she'd also had visions of several historical deaths connected to the collection, as well. Now he was saying there were three more deaths in the present, two more than she'd known about….

She hesitated too long. The front door flew open and there was her mother coming at them, pushing the silver-streaked dark hair from her still pretty face, which was lit by a big welcoming smile.

"You didn't say a thing about bringing a date, Flanna," Delia McKenna said, giving her daughter a hug and kiss on the cheek. "And isn't he a handsome boyo."

"Ma, please—"

Michael smiled in return and a dimple popped in his right cheek. "Why, thank you, Mrs. McKenna."

"An American, is it?"

"Irish-American. Michael Eagan. I can see where your daughter gets her beauty."

Flanna gaped as the private investigator turned on the charm and took her mother's hand. Her mother actually giggled.

"We'll be so pleased to have you as our guest."

"Give us a minute," Flanna said, biting the inside of her cheek when her mother raised her eyebrows and smiled before retreating to the house. She counted silently to three, then faced Michael. "What do you think you're doing?"

"Trying to be pleasant to your mother."

"Now she thinks you and I are—are…"

"Lovers?"

"I was going to say together!"

"You have a problem with intimacy?" One dark eyebrow shot up in challenge.

"I have a problem with you. Perhaps you should leave now and we can meet back in town later."

"You realize if I don't come inside with you, you'll have to explain why."

He had a point. The last thing she wanted to do was further upset her parents, especially her father, with his heart condition and all. They knew about Bridget, of course, and were already troubled about her involvement with the situation. She didn't want to have to explain what Michael Eagan was doing and why he had followed her, because he seemed to think she was somehow suspect in the crime. She didn't want her da having another heart attack.

She had no choice but to go along with the charade for the

moment. "You may come inside with me on one condition, Michael Eagan."

"And what would that be?"

"Say nothing about the thefts or murders. I don't want my family vexed for nothing."

"I wouldn't equate murder to nothing."

"They have no involvement in the crimes. Nor do I, other than as an innocent bystander," she informed him.

Michael nodded. "All right. On your terms. How do we explain who I am and our...relationship?"

"I'll think of something. Just follow my lead," she said, her voice mournful as she turned to go inside.

The fates were conspiring against her.

Once inside, she dipped her fingers into the font of holy water at the door and made the sign of the cross, all the while asking Himself for help.

She was going to have to convince her family that she liked this Michael Eagan, when the only reason he was here was because he thought she knew something about Bridget's death.

Chapter Two

The noisy sounds of blathering and laughter receded as Michael studied his quarry, who was now cutting big chunks of birthday cake and handing them around the table. To be factual, there were twin cakes in the shape of the number three because Flanna McKenna was thirty-three years old today.

He thought she looked younger.

Innocent.

But he wasn't one to be fooled.

Whatever her age, whatever her intentions, the woman certainly had an appeal he couldn't deny. Her strawberry-blond hair was pulled back from her heart-shaped face and caught in a clip at the nape of her lovely neck, from which hung a silver infinity knot studded with what looked like a large chunk of amber. Fine strands skittered over her high cheekbones and along earrings that matched the necklace. Pieces of jewelry she'd designed?

Before realizing what he was doing, he focused on her bowed mouth that promised kisses to send a man reeling. Then he jerked away his gaze and met her eyes, which were a green as vivid and as soft as the rolling countryside, and he was immediately drawn in.

For a moment he forgot why he was there, forgot the murders and thefts and the fact that Barry Rafferty had practically accused Flanna of setting up the heist and therefore being responsible for his mother's death. Instead he appreciated the woman whose curves were hugged by a silky, amber-colored material, the dress having a tight bodice and flowing skirt.

"Cake?" she asked, and he realized she'd been holding out a plate in his direction.

He took it from her similarly silver-and-amber-decorated hand with a curt "Thanks."

"So, Michael, what are your intentions toward my cousin?"

This query came from one of the three big lummoxes seated across the table from him. Brothers, they pretty much looked alike with green eyes, dark hair and chiseled faces set in glares aimed at him.

"Tiernan McKenna!" Flanna gave her cousin an indignant glare. "I would appreciate your keeping a civil tongue in your head."

"What? I just want to make sure his intentions are no more than they should be."

"You *are* thirty-three today," his brother reminded her.

"Don't start with me, Cashel."

"Thirty-three days," Aidan singsonged in a low, teasing voice.

"Be glad that you don't have the legacy hanging over your head," she said.

"No," Aidan returned, his voice suddenly tight. "Just a damn curse."

The table went uncomfortably silent for a moment and Michael shifted in his chair. Legacy? Curse? What was that all about? "Thirty-three days until what?" he asked.

Flanna ignored him. "Michael is a business acquaintance," she announced. "I simply invited him today because he's a stranger in our country and was at odds for the day."

"Business, eh?" Flanna's father murmured. James McKenna fixed Michael with a steady gaze. "And what is it exactly that you do?"

"Da!" Flanna cut him off. "Let's not be talking business on today of all days, please."

Hearing a bit of panic in her voice, Michael couldn't help but smile. "Your daughter is right. Today is her special day, after all."

James grunted and settled back in his chair, then dug in to his piece of cake. The three cousins weren't so easily appeased. Michael was aware of their speculative stares as he took a bite of the cake himself.

"Delicious, isn't it?" asked the elderly nun seated next to him, Flanna's great-aunt Marcella.

"Delicious, indeed, Sister."

"Don't worry about the boyos," she said, indicating the three second cousins still giving him the eye. "They all took up being protective of our darling Flanna where her brother Curran left off."

"Something happened to him?"

"Aye. Curran moved to your America. Their sister Keelin did so, as well. He would be in Kentucky, while she's making her home in Chicago." She forked a piece of cake and said, "I wouldn't be surprised if Flanna will be the next to leave us…perhaps for Boston. I would miss her, but think how grand that would be."

The way she was looking at him made Michael wonder if the whole family was delusional with their talk of legends and curses.

Even so, he found he was enjoying himself. It reminded him a bit of his former life when he still had a father and a brother and uncle to care about, and cousins he had a relationship with…before everything went wrong and he made a U-turn in life. Nostalgia might make a man relax, but not Michael. Always convinced the next bad thing was right around the corner, he remained on guard.

He had to keep in mind why he was here, after all.

Flanna took her seat next to him after placing her own cake in front of her. "Don't mind my family. They like to be in my business."

"What is it about this particular birthday?" he asked.

"Nothing."

"It's the McKenna Legacy," her mother piped up. "Within thirty-three days of her thirty-third birthday, Flanna is to meet the man of her heart."

"Ma!"

"Well, it's true. Look at Curran and Keelin. And your cousins, for heaven's sake! They're all happily married, true to Moira's vision for them. Only you and your cousin Quin are left."

"You know I don't believe in Gran's legacy. It's not for me. I mean to say that it was loving of Gran to wish her grand-children the happiness she had…but I have other plans for my life that don't concern finding a husband. Now, can we talk about something else?"

Michael didn't miss the tightness in Flanna's voice or the becoming flush in her cheeks. Because she believed in what she was saying? Or because she didn't and was covering? Whichever reason, she didn't easily hide strong emotions, and that fact would make getting the truth from her possible.

If he ever got her alone to talk about the crimes.

"More cake, Michael?" Delia asked.

"I couldn't, really."

"Ah, go on, now. That piece you ate so quickly was just an appetizer."

In the end, he let her have her way and had a second piece.

The opportunity to be alone with Flanna came quicker than he imagined. Cake finished, Delia demanded the cousins help her clear the table. James took Great-aunt Marcella in hand and helped her to the parlor, and Flanna—prohibited from lifting a finger on her birthday—indicated he should follow her out into the garden.

Michael opened the door for her and set a hand at the small of her back to guide her out, then felt her flesh shiver beneath his palm. She looked up at him, her eyes wide, and for a moment as he stared into their emerald depths, the world stood still. The breath caught in his throat and his heart seemed to stop. Then she blinked and broke the connection, setting the world back in motion.

Flanna moved to a bench beneath a flowering arbor but didn't sit. She seemed tense, on edge. Because she had something to worry about? he wondered.

"Now, we'll be having a few minutes of peace," she said. "What is it you want to know from me?"

Surprised that she was being so direct, he said, "Whether you have any knowledge of the crimes."

Trying to keep her jaw from clenching, she said, "Probably less than you."

"How can that be when you were making copies of Bridget's Celtic jewelry?"

"I worked for the woman. While we got along, I knew my place."

"Which was…?"

Flanna sighed. "In case you haven't noticed, I come from a family that lives in a modest home. Bridget lived in a manor. The difference between us was as simple as the euro. She had an unlimited supply while I…well, I'm dependent on her son paying my fees as outlined by contract or I... Well, never mind then." She sighed again.

"So you needed money."

"Don't we all, now?"

"Some more than others," he said, checking his pocket watch as if for the time. He ran his thumb over the cracked glass and remembered how it had gotten that way. An old sorrow filled him and he slipped the watch back into his trouser pocket. "And some will do anything to get it."

As he well knew from experience with his own family. He'd been on his way down the same crooked road when his father and brother and uncle had paid the price...and suddenly his priorities in life had changed.

"Why don't you just say it straight out," Flanna said. "You think I had something to do with the robbery."

"Barry Rafferty thinks that. I haven't made up my mind as to what I believe."

Rather, his opinion had altered slightly. He felt less inclined to believe it than when he'd first watched Flanna at the cemetery. That innocence he'd sensed seemed genuine.

"Barry Rafferty is an...a man speaking out of grief," Flanna said. "He needs someone to blame and the easiest someone would be me."

"But you are innocent, right?"

"What do you think? I've already told you—"

"Then you'll help me." Michael didn't know where that came from. He hadn't been planning on it, but now it seemed clear to him what he needed to do.

"Help you what?"

"Find the person responsible."

"And how am I to do that?"

Before he could answer, the cousin named Tiernan stuck

his head out the door. "It's Keelin calling from America to wish you a happy birthday."

"We'll finish this later," Flanna muttered, flying toward the house.

Michael felt his pulse speed up as he watched her go. "Not finish," he murmured. "We've only just begun."

"KEELIN, LOVELY of you to call," Flanna said, throwing herself on the small leather sofa in her da's library. All around her were the books she'd read through childhood and beyond. Through them, her da had opened the world to her.

"What else would I be thinking on the anniversary of my only sister's birth?" Keelin asked. "Especially this one."

"Don't be starting now. I've had enough torture from the family."

Keelin laughed. "I imagine our sainted mother is beside herself. Tiernan told me you brought a man to our parents' home."

One who'd made her pulse jump and her mouth go dry when he'd touched her. Not that she would admit any such thing. The American would be here and gone in no time.

"A man, but not mine."

"Good."

"Good? And here I thought you would be like the rest, pushing me to accept Gran's legacy."

"I want that for you, of course, but…"

"But?"

"Tiernan described him to me. This Michael Eagan is trouble, Flanna."

"Don't I know it."

"I'm not talking trouble like you had with Erin Cassidy. I mean real danger."

Ignoring the mention of the man she'd once thought she loved and the way he had so callously used her, Flanna felt her chest tighten and her mouth go dry. "What is it you saw?"

Her sister's gift had to do with dreams—through them, Keelin could see through another's eyes, either a present event or one in the future. Flanna's gift was one of touch, which mainly gave her the ability to use objects to see bits of the past through highly emotional incidents.

"You were in a car with him," Keelin said. "He was driving like a bat out of hell…then you were screaming like a banshee…"

"And?"

"And then Tyler woke me up. Apparently I was screaming, too."

A shiver shot through Flanna, and she forced herself to take a deep breath. Danger…which meant she was going to get involved with the man. God help her. Keelin's dreams were never wrong.

Not wanting to think about more terrible things on top of Bridget's murder, she changed the subject, asked about her brother-in-law and her niece Kelly and Tyler's daughter Cheryl and the rest of her family in Chicago. But though she enjoyed hearing it all, only part of her was listening.

The other part was mulling over Keelin's premonition about her and Michael Eagan and wondering whether or not she could prevent the incident from happening.

SHE WAS STILL wondering if she could circumvent one of Keelin's premonitions when she returned to her tiny one-bedroom cottage. Though her home was in Dublin, she'd rented the place to be near Bridget Rafferty, who'd insisted on overseeing the replication progress personally. Flanna had converted the dining section of the living area as her workroom, complete with drawing board, workbench and kiln.

Michael had tailed her as he had on the way to Lough Danaan, so he was only a few seconds behind her as she left her car and went to the front door. By the time she got it open, he was there, following her inside.

"Have a seat," she said.

Flanna indicated the part of the living area filled with fussy furniture that wasn't to her taste but had come with the rental. Michael sat on the sofa looking too big for the furniture and strangely odd among the floral prints and ruffles. Not wanting to be any closer to himself than she had to be, Flanna took a chair several yards away.

"Now let's get down to business," she said, wanting to get to his intent. "You're an American. What exactly is your involvement here in Ireland?"

"Officially? None. I don't answer to your local police, although I do have connections with Interpol. They're very interested in the fact that I've connected three murders in three different countries."

His voice was deep and mesmerizing but had the strangest accent with flat-sounding vowels. Flanna had to force herself to concentrate on what he was saying. "Start from the beginning, if you will."

"About a month ago, Samuel Holmes came to see me after his daughter Tina was murdered. He's very high on the social register, a regular Boston Brahman. The murder was directly related to the theft of a Celtic belt that he'd given his daughter for her twenty-first birthday."

From inside his suit jacket, he pulled an envelope with a couple of photographs of Celtic design jewelry. He held out the first one for her to see.

Recognizing the pattern on the girdle belt instantly, Flanna nodded. "The same infinity design as on the pieces I worked on. And the same type of fire opal cabochons. I can't say for sure without seeing the actual pieces, but my guess would be they are from the same collection."

"I thought so. Unfortunately, the Boston police had no leads. No trace evidence at the scene. Though how that could be, I have no idea."

"Possibly through some kind of cover spell cast by the thief." Realizing he was frowning at her, Flanna quickly said, "Go on."

She should have known better than to say something he would no doubt think was blarney.

"My partners and I have worked very hard to build Beacon Hill Investigations. This is the most important case we've been hired to resolve. I thought if I could solve the Holmes murder when the police couldn't…"

"I see. And what made you think you could if there was no evidence of any kind?"

"Connections," he said. "From a past life."

Flanna frowned and stared at him with new intensity. Was he saying that he had once been a criminal himself?

That didn't make sense.

A record would preclude his being licensed as a private investigator. And her from working with him. One criminal mixed up in her life was enough for any sane woman.

"That makes it sound like you have a personal interest," she said carefully.

"Only as to wanting to see justice done. I didn't know the Holmes girl or her father before he hired me. But I understand his grief, his need for resolution. Too many never get that. If I can give that to him…"

Flanna relaxed. It *was* personal for him, but not in the way she had feared. No matter his denial, he had a vested interest in solving this case. She wondered what drove him, what terrible thing had happened to him in the past to make him leave his own country in pursuit of a lead. Whatever it was, it humanized him. She felt drawn to help him and not just because she'd known Bridget.

"Even with connections, I couldn't get a lead in Boston," he went on, his tone fraught with tension. "No one knew anything about the murder or the theft. The belt was very valuable, and yet the thief didn't try to fence it. There was no talk on the street whatsoever. I was at an impasse for weeks, when there was a report of a similar murder in London in the theft of a brooch of Celtic design. The victim was Sally Easton. She left behind a husband and three kids."

He held out the second photograph, this one printed on thinner paper, as though he'd copied it from an article on the Internet. There was no denying the similarities.

"They do look to be the missing pieces to the suite," Flanna agreed. "The Raffertys have the rest."

"Had," Michael said, emphasizing the past tense. "Now the murderer has it all."

"Not all."

"That's right." His expression intense, he said, "Barry Rafferty claimed you still have several pieces that belonged to his mother."

"And he'll have them and the replicas in his possession after he has his bank cut me a check on Monday."

"You keep them here?"

Flanna gripped the arms of her chair. "They're someplace safe," she said, not wanting to reveal any details.

As if she would tell him where to find the other pieces. No matter his selfless intentions on chasing the lead to Ireland, how did she know Michael hadn't made an agreement to return the pieces in her possession to Barry Rafferty?

"If they're here, you could be putting yourself in danger," he said.

Softening toward him once more, she shrugged. "I haven't worn the real pieces." Though she had tried on the replicas.

"What does that have to do with anything?"

"Why, I wouldn't go against the curse, of course."

"Curse?"

Uh-oh, now she'd done it. The way he was looking at her…he thought she was crazy. Oh, well. She might as well tell him. "Other women have died for Caillech's treasures."

"More than three murders?"

"Call them what you will. I'm sure you must know the history of the collection."

"I did my research. I know the jewelry was made in the Middle Ages and that it was stolen from the rightful owner."

"Caillech was a powerful sorceress who was burned at the stake by an envious English noblewoman who wanted the jewelry for herself because she thought it would give her powers," Flanna clarified. "As Caillech burned, she cursed the woman who condemned her and anyone else throughout time who wore her treasures. They would then die. And it's said that if anyone wears the entire suite on Beltane—May first and the day she died—the sorceress will return in that person's form, linking her powers with that person forever."

"Yes, yes, I read that, too. The whole thing is an interesting myth."

"It's more than a myth."

"Well, you really have no way of knowing that."

"But I do. I've seen it."

"Seen what?"

A beat of silence turned into an uncomfortable moment as Flanna considered what she would tell Michael. Then, again, perhaps Barry had already expressed his opinion. The eldest Rafferty sibling surely thought she was mad.

"The deaths," Flanna finally said, knowing that if they were to work together, she had to be up front. And she was going to work with him, both to get justice for Bridget and to prevent other deaths. "When I touched the originals. I have a… My grandmother called it a gift." She knew telling him was like speaking to a wall. He would take in her words but they would slide away from him. And yet she needed to be honest. "When I touch objects, sometimes I can see things…. Things that happened in the past when high emotions were involved."

"Barry Rafferty suggested you would come up with some wild story."

Flanna took a deep breath and told herself to stay calm. Michael only knew her from the other man's point of view. "Yes, Barry is not fond of anyone with the name McKenna." As he had made clear to her at the grave site that very morning.

"And why would that be?"

"I'm sure because he doesn't believe in what he cannot see or touch. My Grandmother Moira was a *bean feasa,* with what some call magical powers—various psychic abilities and the healing touch, as well. She was well-known in this part of the country. Her grandchildren inherited their gifts from her. We all have different parts of her in us. My cousin Skelly is the only one who didn't actually inherit something you would call strange. He inherited Gran's gift of storytelling, which is equally important to the Irish."

As she rushed through her explanation, Flanna could see Michael disengage as if he were waiting for her to run out of steam.

She didn't know why it felt so important that he should understand. Maybe it was the attraction she was trying to ignore. She didn't need anyone to make her happy, but that didn't mean she couldn't appreciate a fine-looking man, even one as vexing as Michael Eagan. Besides which, they had a common interest in finding the murdering thief that had taken three women's lives.

"So you touched these pieces and saw women die for them?" Michael didn't make any effort to cover the skeptical note in his question.

"The first was in the court of Elizabeth the First. She wore the earrings and was poisoned. A horrible, painful death." Flanna shuddered at the memory. "The second was someplace in Spain. A flamenco dancer wore the ring while performing. She was attacked on the way home."

"Very colorful visions."

Prompted by grave emotional stakes. Flanna didn't know why that was so—that some kind of danger in the past needed to be involved for her gift to kick in—but there it was.

"Shall I go on?" she asked.

"No need. I get the drift."

Nothing in him said he believed. So why did that disappoint her so?

He said, "Tina Holmes, Sally Easton and Bridget Rafferty were all killed within a month's time. That can't be coincidence. Some private collector obviously will go to any lengths to get what he wants. Which includes murder, and has nothing to do with any curse."

Disappointed if not surprised, Flanna sighed. "If you don't respect what I have to say, then perhaps there's no need for you to be here."

Michael's visage darkened, but he kept his voice even as he asked, "Are you willing to allow a murderer to go free?"

"Not if I can help. I said I was willing to work with you." For Bridget and the other victims. For him, too, Flanna admitted to herself. There was something about Michael Eagan that moved her, despite his natural skepticism to what he didn't understand. She sensed a wound in him that drove him, that made solving this murder case more than a matter of money or fame for his agency. "I'm trying the only way I know how."

The question was…would using her gift as an investigative tool be something he would choose to accept?

IT WAS DARK by the time the American investigator left the McKenna woman's home. He opened the door of his rental car, climbed behind the wheel and started the engine. A moment later, he was moving off.

Time to act.

But wait. What the hell was the bastard doing?

Rather than heading for some inn, Eagan did a U-turn and parked his car smack against the nearby hedgerow, his windshield facing the house, giving him a clear view not only of the front door, but also the gate to the back. Then he cut the engine and the lights and sank down in the seat as if making himself comfortable.

For the night?

Bloody hell!

The few remaining pieces of the Celtic collection were still inside that cottage with only a woman to see to them. No challenge there. But now it appeared she had a guardian angel. It seemed near impossible to get the goods with the man to provide protection.

Violence was now a given, and not just to the woman and her defender…unless Flanna McKenna could be gotten alone.

Chapter Three

The next morning as Flanna and Michael set off for Rafferty Manor, she asked, "How long did you wait before you knocked me up?"

Seeming startled, Michael asked, "What?"

"When I put the kettle on the boil for tea," she said, watching him closely, "I peered out the kitchen window and saw your car parked at the hedgerow. That was quite a bit before you came to the door."

His hands tightened on the steering wheel—the only sign that she'd perturbed him.

His voice was even as he said, "I realized I got to your place a little too early and decided to wait before disturbing you."

Not believing such blarney, Flanna turned her attention away from him and to the road that rolled in dips and curves. Rafferty Manor itself rose above the estuary—the confluence of the River Shannon and the Atlantic Ocean—on a gentle bluff, making it look like something out of a fairy tale.

Suddenly she asked, "How long did you wait?"

"Awhile."

Flanna pierced him with a steady gaze, as if that would get

the truth from him. "How long is *awhile* in Irish time? Minutes? Hours?" Pausing a second, she added, "All night?" She knew he'd been spying on her. "You *are* wearing the same shirt from yesterday. I recognize the little smudge on the sleeve. Birthday cake frosting."

A sound of irritation that was something like a growl was followed by his saying, "What if I traveled without a change of clothing?"

"Is that what happened?" she asked coolly. Playing verbal games had never appealed to her.

"Look, I thought you needed watching!"

"Afraid I would run with the remaining pieces, were you?"

"I was afraid you weren't safe."

A very different thing, indeed, she realized. Sniffing, she gave him the benefit of the doubt—that he had been looking out for her best interests.

Michael glanced at her, but dark glasses covered his eyes, and she couldn't read him. Still, she heard a note of sincerity in his words as he continued.

"You aren't, you know. Not safe. Not until you give up the last of the original pieces."

"You've decided I'm not the guilty one, then?"

That should be of some comfort, Flanna guessed, as they swung off through tall iron gates and onto the estate road.

So why wasn't she comfortable with Michael Eagan?

She hadn't committed any crime, but she could understand he needed to be sure.

Why did he have her so on edge?

"I've decided the odds are against your being involved, Flanna. In thinking on it, I figured you could have taken whatever the Rafferty woman gave you and disappeared weeks or months ago. Of course, you could have been trying to throw off the authorities," he added, "but I had your where-abouts checked out. They assured me that for the last month you were living right here."

"You do consider all possibilities."

"That's my job. Everyone is suspect until I have reason to believe otherwise. I'm very good at what I do."

"As am I."

Certain he knew she was referring to her gift, Flanna wasn't surprised that he said nothing. No reassurances there. No scoffing at her, either. Perhaps he was content to wait and see. Or he was simply weary of being at odds with her.

Whatever his suspicions were, Flanna's only concern was finding the bastard who'd murdered Bridget in cold blood and seeing that justice was done, no matter the cost to herself.

"My remaining tight in one place doesn't preclude my in-volvement, though," she mused. "I could have an accomplice."

"Are you trying to make me think you're guilty?"

"I'm simply considering all the possibilities. You did consider that one, did you not?"

"Of course I did. No need to be sarcastic."

Perhaps there wasn't.

As Michael pulled his rental car onto the long drive that was a tunnel of greenery transporting them to a different world, Flanna tried to relax. Coming here to speak to the servants had been her idea, one he'd readily accepted. Servants normally knew everything that was going on in the house. Normally they were discreet, as well. But whether their giving the *garda* nothing to go on was a matter of dis-cretion or of the wrong questions being asked or because they really didn't know anything of value, Flanna wasn't certain.

Michael was looking at this situation from a different perspective. He'd been investigating since the first murder, so perhaps he would be able to get answers where the local authorities could not.

And perhaps she would get answers, as well, in her own way. Not a plan that she had shared with Michael, of course. She hadn't wanted to start the investigation with an argument, so she'd kept her purpose to herself.

If she learned anything of value, *then* she would have something to say.

As they pulled up close to the manor and peered through the windshield at the turrets, Michael whistled. "Quite a place. I assume the whole family lives here?"

"Not all. Well, all have quarters here, I'm sure, but Katie lives in Dublin, Barry's work is in Galway, so he has a city home there, and Eamon recently bought a much smaller estate in the next town over."

"This place looks big enough for anyone to have privacy. The younger son didn't get along with his mother?"

"Something to ask those in the know, now, is it not?"

Walking up the drive, they passed a silver Bentley and a red Porsche, and a sombre-looking Katie Rafferty was just getting into a black Mercedes.

Once more, Flanna's heart went out to the young woman who blamed herself for her mother's death.

Before they reached the porch, the double front doors opened. Hugh Nolan, Rafferty Manor's houseman—he detested the title of butler, Bridget had told her—stood there. Middle age suited the man, gave his ordinary face character and threaded his thick, dark hair with silver. Though he was a bit shorter than Michael, Hugh appeared equally fit. Not an unattractive man, Flanna thought.

"Miss Flanna, good morning." His gray gaze on her was

steady, but when he looked to Michael, one eyebrow rose in a questioning arch.

"Good morning, Hugh. This would be Mr. Michael Eagan from Boston in America. He's investigating another theft and murder related to Mrs. Rafferty's. I said I would help him any way I could and thought perhaps the way to start would be with the staff here. *If* his talking with them is agreeable with you, of course."

"Of course. Mr. Barry spoke of you, sir. Come in."

He led them to a parlor with a view of the estuary, a big room with deep red walls and a large fireplace with a carved wooden mantel. A few small mahogany tables, a desk and a cabinet reflected the past, but the room was appointed with contemporary couches and overstuffed upholstered chairs.

"Only the housekeeper and groundsman are here presently," Hugh said. "The rest of the staff was told not to return until notified by Mr. Barry."

"It's a start," Michael said. "And perhaps we can get names and addresses of those who aren't here, as well."

Hugh nodded. "Of course. Give me a moment." He turned to a desk with a telephone.

Michael was examining the painting over the fireplace. "It looks like a real O'Keeffe."

"Indeed," Flanna said, admiring the Georgia O'Keeffe painting with its New Mexico influence, "'tis the original."

His gaze swept the room, pausing on other objects of value—a sculpture and a silver tea set among them. "I realize that our thief had a specific goal in mind, but it's hard to believe he would leave behind articles worth so much money."

"If money was the object."

"Right. A private collector only interested in specific pieces might neglect the rest."

"Especially if the objective was merely to gain the collection's power."

Before Michael could respond to her supernatural reference, Hugh said, "Margaret and Frederick will be here presently. In the meantime, if you have questions for me…"

"Certainly. Why don't we sit."

Michael made himself comfortable in one of the overstuffed chairs. Flanna remained mobile, waiting for an opportunity to slip out of the room.

"Did Mrs. Rafferty ever complain about anyone wanting something from her?"

"Miss Bridget was not one to complain," Hugh said. "She kept a positive attitude. She trusted everyone."

"Trusted… Any thoughts on that?"

"She never thought ill of anyone, no matter what."

"Should she have?" Flanna asked.

"There were times when she could have been more…well, circumspect," Hugh admitted.

Michael asked, "With whom? Friends? Children?"

"She was very supportive of her children."

"Were they supportive of her? I understand none of them wanted to stay in this house with her."

Impressed with the way Michael worked in that point so effortlessly, Flanna slid closer to the doorway, even as the housekeeper entered.

"Miss Kate's work is in Dublin," Hugh said. "And Mr. Barry's is in Galway."

"What about the younger brother, Eamon? I understand he bought a place nearby."

Hugh hesitated a moment before saying, "That was a concern for Miss Bridget."

"A monetary concern?"

"You understand that I and the rest of the staff are dependent on the goodwill of the family."

"I won't reveal you as my source, Hugh, no matter what you tell me."

The houseman nodded. His expression earnest, he said, "Mr. Eamon had some trouble managing his finances. Miss Bridget had to assist."

Flanna was about to slip away when Margaret moved closer to the men, saying, "Why not be saying it like it is? She paid his way like always. He could waste his money on anything and everything and she would step up for him. No sense of responsibility, that one."

Trusting that Michael would share anything he learned with her later, Flanna quietly slipped out of the room and quickly headed for the staircase. She needed to get in Bridget's room, to inspect the scene of the crime. Alone. Not that she would be looking for tangible clues. What she might learn through her gift of touch would be inadmissable as any kind of evidence, but it could give her something to put Michael's investigation on the right track.

Flanna knew that Bridget kept Caillech's treasures in her bedroom, though where exactly, she wasn't certain. She'd never actually seen her remove it from a safe. But when she'd come to collect the pieces to make the duplicates, Bridget had given them to her in the bedroom.

Finding the right door, Flanna stopped for a moment and took a deep breath. Using her touch wasn't an easy thing for her. She not only saw things, but felt them as well. She'd experienced the horror and shock and pain of the other women who'd been killed for pieces of the jewelry suite, and she had to be prepared to do the same today.

Quickly, she opened the door and entered. The rooms

looked as she remembered them—a lavish and serene place to get away from the day's tribulations.

Ironic that its occupant was killed right here, in what she'd considered her safe place.

Flanna circled the sleeping area, slowly running her hand over the bed and nightstands, hoping to feel the energy that would give her entry to the past. Nothing. She touched the paintings on the wall; perhaps one was hiding the safe. Nothing there, either. She continued following the wall through the sitting room, the closet and the bath, touching every object she saw.

Nothing, nothing, nothing.

Returning to the bedroom itself, she paused as she took in two dressers, a dressing table and another painting, a portrait of Bridget herself when she was young. Her pulse fluttered and her gaze narrowed on the dressing table. She sat before it, ran her hand over the surface, over the pots of potions and scents, across the brushes and fancy hair-clips.

Nothing. And yet, she couldn't tear herself away.

What was it about the dressing table? If it had something to say to her, why didn't it? Perhaps she was touching the wrong area.

No sooner had Flanna considered that thought, than she realized Bridget might have used the dressing table to hold her treasures. She opened each drawer but found only practical toiletry articles and felt nothing at all.

Still, she couldn't tear herself away. Something was keeping her glued to the spot.

What if there was a hidden compartment?

The table itself seemed awfully thick not to have a drawer in the middle. And there was an unused area above both sets of drawers that could hide a slim hidden space, as well.

Mouth dry in anticipation, she felt under the table. When

her fingers skimmed the area toward the wall, they bumped against metal. Her heart thudded faster. This was it. The release.

Preparing herself mentally for the emotional ride, Flanna pressed the trigger. With a whisper, a hidden, velvet-lined drawer slid out from one side just under the tabletop.

Flanna could hardly breathe. This was the hiding place. She was certain. Fingers trembling, she reached for the interior. As she connected, an electrical charge jumped up to kiss her flesh.

Then she was lost…

"I can't believe you would steal from me!"

Bridget's expression went from fury to something softer, something more cruel altogether.

Horror tore through Flanna as she recognized Bridget's fate.

A blur of motion arced toward the woman's head—a dark-gloved hand holding a silver candlestick. A solid thunk preceded Bridget's sharp cry. She rocked on her feet and, with a choked gasp, tumbled to the floor.

Flanna gasped and her head swam as she started to come out of the vision. She fought the shift…fought to stay in the past…squeezed her eyes shut and concentrated on the body crumpled on the floor.

The killer turned back to the dressing table…grabbed up silver-and-bronze Celtic pieces…stuffed them into a half-empty velvet bag…

Flanna willed the murderer to look in the mirror, willed him to let her see something, anything that would identify him. But the only thing crowding her vision was…

The gloved hand lifted the velvet pouch.

The glove… What was that marking at the wrist?

The murderer started to leave, then stood over Bridget as if mourning her….

"What the hell are you doing in here?"

With a jerk, Flanna came out of the trance. Weak and dazed as she always was after using her gift, she had trouble focusing on the man storming into the room.

"Bloody hell!" Barry said even more vehemently. "What are you doing in my mother's room?"

"I—I was trying to see…."

Breathless, legs shaking, Flanna gripped the back of the dressing table chair as a wave of nausea coursed through her. She would be all right. She just needed a few minutes to recover.

"How dare you. You have no right to be here, not without asking my permission." Barry's voice rose as she refused to answer. "Or maybe you didn't want permission because you were snooping around, thinking to loot Mother's valuables!"

"No, of course not."

"Then why are you here?" Barry demanded.

"Because I thought I could help." Flanna took a deep breath, and even knowing he wouldn't believe her, said, "I saw the murder."

"What? You were here when my mother died and you've said nothing about it for days?"

Just then, a rattled Hugh Nolan entered the room, Michael following close behind.

"Are you all right?" Michael asked, his expression one of concern as he stepped closer to her and placed a steadying hand on her arm.

Though she nodded, she really wasn't all right. She could use a sit and a cup of cool water. But at least she had backup, she thought as Michael pulled closer as if to support her physically.

Still, Flanna tried to explain. "I meant I saw her murder just now. That's why I wanted to search your mother's rooms, so I could use my gift to help. I touched the drawer where she'd hidden the collection—" she indicated the still-open secret compartment in the dressing table "—and saw the candlestick come down on her head."

"How do you know about the candlestick?" Barry went so red-faced he seemed almost apoplectic. "The authorities have kept that information from being released."

"As I just told you," Flanna said, "I saw it happen in my vision."

"V-vision?" Barry sputtered.

"I think it's time we left." Michael placed an arm around her shoulders and encouraged her to move toward the door. To Barry he said, "Sorry if we overstepped bounds in our investigation, but I'm sure you appreciate we are trying to find your mother's murderer."

"The *gardai* will do that!" When they moved off, Barry shouted after them, "And don't be surprised if that chit is playing you and is involved, after all."

Glad to be away from the awful man, Flanna leaned into Michael. It was good to have someone solid there. It always took her a bit to recover from the emotional force of her visions and she doubted she could manage the stairs alone just yet. With him at her side, his arm steadying her, she didn't have to. Her knees were still wobbly, her pulse still surging through her. She melted against him for a moment.

But the moment didn't last long.

For when halfway down the stairs, he whispered, "Are you crazy?" she stiffened.

"Not to my knowledge."

"Then why are you acting like it? Did you really want to convince Barry Rafferty you're touched by telling such a wild tale?"

"Perhaps that's my purpose," she said, pulling away from him. "To make everyone think I'm mad."

Chapter Four

They left Rafferty Manor and walked out into a thick fog rising from the riverbank, smothering the rolling land of the estate.

Uneasy, Flanna said, "Perhaps I should drive."

"That won't be necessary."

Michael's words held a note of finality about them that brooked no argument. And yet, she couldn't help herself.

"You don't know the roads—"

"I've been driving for years now in all kinds of conditions. I can manage."

"They're tricky in weather."

"Which presents no problem since I'm that good a driver." He opened the door for her. "Do you always need to have control of everything?"

Clenching her jaw, Flanna slid into the passenger seat, settled back and tried to relax as Michael took the wheel. Though it was still morning, the sky had darkened and the fog was as thick as pea soup. As they set off, a thrill shot through her, and a tight ball of unease settled in her stomach as a residual effect.

Taking a deep breath, Flanna figured there was only one way to calm herself—she needed to talk, to get her irritation out in the open.

"I really did see the murder."

The statement was met by silence.

"Do you want to hear this or not?" she asked.

"If you must."

Grand. He was humoring her.

They whipped through the tunnel of greenery that brought them back to the estate entry. Michael barely slowed as he turned onto the road. Not that he was driving really fast— just too fast for the weather and Flanna's taste. The headlights were on, and the beams cut through the fog and then abruptly dropped off. She didn't see the car coming from the other direction until both swerved slightly as they passed each other.

A quick glance at Michael told her he wasn't as unnerved as she was. If she warned him to be careful, he would no doubt be further annoyed.

Not that talking about her vision would be any more well-received. Still, she had to convince him that she'd really *had* a vision.

"We're working together, Michael," she finally said. "We have a common goal. You shouldn't so easily dismiss what I saw in my vision."

"Then tell me."

The words were right, but his tone wasn't. He really didn't want to hear, undoubtedly because he wasn't prepared to believe her crazy story as he no doubt thought of it.

"Bridget came upon her murderer in the midst of the theft," she said anyway.

"No surprise there."

"She *was* surprised, not just that someone would steal from her…but someone she knew."

"She said that? A name?"

Was he actually accepting her story? Flanna warmed up to the tale. "Bridget said, 'I can't believe you would steal from me,' as if she knew the thief. And her expression…it went beyond anger or fear."

"What else is there?"

Seeing the woman's crushed expression in her mind's eye, Flanna said, "Betrayal."

"Is that all you have?"

So she hadn't made him a believer, after all. Glancing into the side-view mirror, she saw another set of headlights cut through the fog behind them.

"If only I could have seen more. As it was, I got a glimpse only of a hand holding the candlestick and later the velvet bag with the stolen treasure."

"Then we don't know anything more than before you searched her room."

"Did you not hear me? She *knew* her killer."

Another glance into the side mirror nearly blinded her— headlights from the vehicle behind them were closing in. Too closely for the conditions.

"Bridget knew a lot of people," Michael said. "They all attended her funeral."

"Someone she was close to," Flanna insisted. That had been betrayal Bridget was feeling, she knew it. "If only I could have made out the insignia on the glove."

"What?"

"The hand I saw was gloved and there was some marking on the wrist."

"That's really helpful."

Michael's sarcastic tone made her clench her jaw. "Don't believe me, then."

Suddenly the headlights from behind shot sideways and

Flanna glanced back to see a dark car swerve around to the right. The fog was too thick to see details.

"He's trying to go around you in this fog!"

"So I noticed." Michael's hands tightened on the steering wheel.

She squinted through the fog to get her bearings. "If I'm not mistaken, there's a curve just up ahead. And a dangerous drop-off." Then she glanced over to the passing car to see it move closer to the Renault. The road had no shoulder to speak of. If Michael weren't careful, they would be too close to the edge.

Suddenly he gunned the Renault and pulled away in a burst of speed. Flanna glanced back and saw the other headlights recede, but only slightly. The other driver was no doubt angry that he hadn't been allowed to pass and was keeping pace with them.

Thankfully, they quickly passed the drop-off and started descending. They were almost through the part of the road that presented a series of dips and curves. Michael zigzagged and came out along a straight strip now lined with a hedgerow. The other vehicle still stuck too close behind.

"Bloody hell," she muttered. "I think the other driver is out for revenge."

Suddenly another set of headlights came at them from the front—a lorry of some size.

"Watch out!" she yelled, heart in her throat.

Michael swerved, narrowly squeezing between the over-sized vehicle and the hedgerow. The lorry wobbled, then straightened, coming back across the center of the road. Flanna looked back in time to see the other vehicle swerve also—directly into the hedgerow, where it became mired in a wet bog.

"That was close!"

"Too close," Michael said, his voice tight.

Glancing back, Flanna saw the lorry stop and the driver alight from the cab, but what happened next was lost in the fog.

As they approached Killarra, the fog thinned and then disappeared altogether. The day was still gray, the air fine with drizzle, but at least the dangerous weather lay behind them. They were headed for St. Mary's and a Sunday afternoon Mass with the hopes that afterward, Father O'Reilly could tell them something to help their investigation.

Something not learned under the seal of the confessional, Flanna thought.

Michael remained silent. Either he really did think she was crazy or that she was making up the story about seeing Bridget's death. His lack of interest after she'd recounted the entire vision seared her.

She should have known better than to tell a stranger, anyway.

Erin Cassidy had taught her a valuable lesson, one she should have remembered.

Erin had been everything an impressionable young woman could want in a young man...or so Flanna had thought when she'd met him five years before. He'd been easy to look at, easy to get to know, despite the fact that he didn't have the kind of career drive of other men she'd dated. She hadn't cared. Erin had been fun. He'd loved her psychic ability and had encouraged her to test it at every turn.

But he'd simply been using her.

Flanna shifted in her seat. What was she doing thinking about the worst mistake she'd ever made? A mistake that had been personal, and nothing whatsoever to do with Michael Eagan.

"Here we are." Michael pulled into the church parking lot. After exiting, he circled to her door and then just stood there for a moment, looking around as though he was expecting trouble. He finally opened the door for her, then held out his hand. "You don't mind being seen with me, I assume."

Ignoring his offer of help, Flanna slid out unaided. "I would think it's you who would mind being seen with me."

"Not at all. I always enjoy having a lovely lass on my arm."

There he went with the charm, and after making her feel so irritable a short while ago. The smile he aimed at her was blazing in its intensity as he held out that very arm.

"There'll be no touching," she said, again avoiding him.

"Hmm, no touching, no intimacy. You are a difficult woman to get to know, Flanna McKenna."

She paused and said, "Think of me as a partner, not a woman."

His heavy gaze slowly worked its way down her body. "That would be very difficult, indeed."

Flustered, Flanna turned and headed for the church door. Once inside, she recognized a few of the townspeople that had preceded them. No Raffertys, thankfully. And no Lisa Madden, which was something of a disappointment. She'd hoped to talk to the woman about Bridget, but obviously Lisa had gone to early-morning Mass. They would have to catch up with her afterward at home.

Flanna felt watched by the townspeople sprinkled throughout the small church. No doubt they were wondering about Michael. The pew felt crowded with him so close to her, and she had a difficult time keeping her attention where it belonged. Her family's fault, she thought, for bringing up Gran's legacy the day before. And the way he'd looked her over before coming inside had certainly made her pulse race. She couldn't help but consider Michael Eagan as a woman considers a man, but she had no intention of fulfilling any prophecy.

Remembering where she was when Father O'Reilly started the Mass, Flanna concentrated on her primary reason for being there. She prayed for Bridget Rafferty's soul and for help in finding whomever had killed the three women.

When the Mass was over, the silver-haired priest stood outside to greet each of his parishioners. Flanna and Michael waited until everyone else had left before approaching him.

"Can we talk to you, Father?" Flanna asked. "About Bridget Rafferty?"

"Of course. Are you wanting to have a Mass said for her?"

"Actually, we need information."

As Flanna introduced Michael and his investigation of the related murders that had led him to Ireland, the priest's visage tightened and his usually smiling mouth turned into a frown. She decided to let Michael handle the interview.

"You think the thefts and murders are all connected then?" the priest asked.

"I do," Michael said.

"You're speaking of an international criminal."

"Who could be right here in Killarra, Father." Michael used his most respectful tone. "Someone who knows the worth of the collection. A collector or a person of interest who is acquainted with him and is willing to do anything for the money that the complete Celtic suite will bring."

"Then how can I help?" Father O'Reilly seemed genuinely bewildered. "I know of no one like that."

"Maybe not, but maybe you do. Apparently Bridget's son is desperate for money."

"Oh, come now, Barry may have a weakness for the horses and get himself in deeper than he means to, but he wouldn't do anything illegal. And he certainly wouldn't see a hair on his mother's head harmed."

Flanna and Michael looked at each other. So both brothers

had money troubles? Interesting. Despite the priest's claim, was one of the brothers desperate enough to kill to solve his financial difficulties?

Flanna finally spoke up. "Michael meant Eamon, Father."

The priest coughed and said, "I wouldn't be knowing anything about that now. Not anything I could say."

That comment meant Bridget had told Father O'Reilly about Eamon's financial situation under the seal of the confessional. For some reason, the mother hadn't wanted her younger son's money troubles to be public knowledge. Flanna knew that no matter how long they had with Father O'Reilly, he wasn't going to talk about Eamon.

Apparently the older brother was a different story. Because Barry's financial difficulties weren't serious? Or because his mother hadn't known about them and neither had spoken of them in the confessional?

As if they were on the same page, Michael said, "So Barry plays the ponies. How seriously?"

"I wouldn't know that." Now the priest looked truly uncomfortable. "Perhaps I shouldn't be saying anything at all about himself."

To Flanna, Father O'Reilly's admission meant Barry's love affair with thoroughbreds might be serious, indeed.

"I can leave it to the authorities to ask you," Michael said.

The priest stiffened. "Which would be for the best then."

Realizing Father O'Reilly felt offended, Flanna took Michael's arm, and said, "Thank you for your time, Father. Sorry to be bothering you." Then she tugged Michael away.

"I thought there was to be no touching," he murmured.

Instantly Flanna released him. "You didn't need to put him off. I thought you were good at what you do."

"He knew something he wasn't saying."

"You should have played the charm card rather than threatening him with the *gardai*."

To that Michael had no response.

Once in the car, he asked, "Where to now?"

"Straight to the center of town to find Lisa Madden. She and Bridget were best friends. She owns an interior design business and has an apartment right above."

"A design business in a small town like Killarra?"

"Apparently big-city people aren't the only ones who want to live surrounded by nice things." Realizing she was being too prickly, she added, "Lisa doesn't limit her clients to Killarra. She has quite a following." Or so Bridget had told her.

Two minutes later, they parked in front of Madden Interiors. The lights in the shop were on.

"Good, I see her inside," Flanna said, leading the way.

Though Madden Interiors wasn't open for business on a Sunday, the front door was unlocked and Lisa was at her drawing table, colored pencils in hand. When she looked up, her surprise was written on her face.

"Flanna. What are you doing here? Have you decided to stay, then, and fix up the cottage?"

"Actually we're here to talk to you about Bridget. This is Michael Eagan from Boston in America."

"An American? What interest would you have in a murdered Irishwoman?"

Michael quickly explained.

"Oh, my." Seeming agitated, Lisa stood and moved away from her work area. "This is the first I've heard of other murders. Are the local authorities aware of your investigation?"

Michael nodded. "Interpol, as well."

"Well, then, what can I do to help?"

Flanna said, "I thought since you were Bridget's best

friend, you would be the one to know if she was having difficulties with anyone."

"Bridget? She was the soul of kindness. She never wished anyone ill. Never gave anyone trouble."

"But what about others?" Michael asked. "Did she fear her kindness wasn't reciprocated?"

"Not exactly."

"Which means?"

"No one had it in for her. Not that I know of."

"Then what?"

"Well, she was concerned about Eamon. She feared he'd gotten himself involved with what you Americans call a loan shark when she refused him money a few months back. Bridget said it was that friend of Eamon's—Sean Hogan—who got him in trouble by encouraging him to seek out an unconventional way of paying his debts. She never did trust Sean. He's been trouble since he was old enough to know what money was for."

"A thief?" Michael asked.

Lisa nodded. "Among other things. Mostly petty crimes, but still he knows the inside of a lock-up."

"What are you saying exactly?" Michael asked.

Now Lisa was looking distinctly uncomfortable. "I'm not making any accusations, mind you."

"But you think we should look into this Sean Hogan?"

"Someone should. I told the detective on the case about him, but he didn't seem to think Sean was a factor."

"Which means he probably didn't talk to the man," Michael said. "An omission I intend to correct. Can you tell me where to find this Hogan?"

"I don't know where he lives, but you could try Garrity's pub. Bridget once said he spent all his time there. She was afraid Eamon would start doing the same."

"We'll look in to it."

As they were about to go out the door, Lisa placed a hand on Michael's arm and said, "Thank you."

"For what?"

"For caring enough to want justice for Bridget. I can tell that this is more than a paycheck for you."

Michael smiled, patted her hand and carefully extracted himself. Flanna waited until they were almost to the car to comment.

"Lisa is insightful. I've had the same feeling about you. So what makes you tick, Michael Eagan? What really brought you here to Ireland?"

"Maybe it is just a paycheck."

"Maybe that's part of it, but I sense there's more. And that's part of why I agreed to work with you in the first place. So will you be telling me your story?"

He opened the passenger door for her. "Maybe someday." The words were casual, but the tightness around his mouth wasn't.

Flanna got in the car, her gaze glued to Michael as he closed the door and circled to the driver's side. Every so often, despite his normally easy smile and charming manner, she sensed a hollowness in him. There indeed was something that drove Michael Eagan, and Flanna suspected he would have to trust her implicitly in order to talk about his past.

Chapter Five

As he started the engine, Michael asked, "Is there anyone you can stay with?"

Confused, Flanna asked, "Why would I want to stay with someone?"

"I would feel better if you weren't alone."

The statement sounded as if he meant to leave her behind. "I'll be with *you*."

"I don't want to put you in an untenable position. Look, Flanna, I think I should go after Sean Hogan alone. He very well might be dangerous. At least that's the impression I got from the Madden woman."

"I trust you to protect me."

He pulled the car out of the lot, saying, "I don't trust myself to do my best job if I'm worried about you."

His expression conveyed that worry. Flanna wasn't used to a man's concern for her welfare, other than her brother's. The idea was touching if misplaced.

"I'm flattered, Michael. But Lisa didn't say this Sean Hogan was violent."

"Chances are he's been locked up with violent criminals more than once. What do you think that does to a man?"

He sounded as if he had personal experience and knew exactly what it might do.

"Isn't there someone?" he asked.

"My home is in Dublin. I've just been here long enough to do the work for Bridget." She'd been so busy, she'd made lots of acquaintances, but not really any friends. "And I can take care of myself."

"Bridget probably thought the same."

"Bridget wasn't forewarned. I am."

Michael heaved a sigh of exasperation. "All right. I'll drop you off at the cottage before I go find Hogan."

"You can drop me off in town at the petrol station. They have a minimart and I need to pick up a few things."

"Then I'll wait and take you home."

"It's not necessary, really. I often walk from town."

"Today you'll ride. And then you'll lock the doors and not open them unless it's me knocking."

Flanna didn't want to make this into a contest of wills. He obviously was convinced he was acting in her best interests.

"Fine."

Who was she to argue? The stress of the day was exhausting enough.

At the minimart, she picked up the few items she needed and let Michael drive her back to the cottage. He made her wait at the door while he went inside to make sure she didn't have a surprise visitor.

Michael's protectiveness might be a bit irritating, but on the other hand, the caring gesture warmed Flanna to him. A man who barely knew her was willing to take responsibility for her, and she guessed that wasn't simply because she could help him. Since Michael didn't believe in her gift, she didn't know of what possible use she could be to him.

Obviously he cared about what happened to others to the extent that he was willing to put himself out for them.

For her.

He was truly an unusual man.

"All clear," he told her when he returned from his house inspection. Pulling out his cell phone, he said, "Let's trade numbers."

"I don't have a cell phone."

"Everyone has a cell phone."

"Not everyone. Not me. I don't want to be found wherever, whenever. I think people rely too much on technology these days. I prefer to rely on nature. I enjoy working with my hands—"

"Fine," he said, cutting her off. "Give me the number of the house phone and I'll give you my cell." After he punched in the number, he wrote his down on a piece of paper and handed it to her. "Keep the windows and doors locked."

"See to yourself," she said, showing him out the door, then dead-bolting it as he'd instructed.

Thankfully tomorrow was Monday. Barry Rafferty would go to the bank and draw her check and she would return Bridget's jewelry and replicas. Then she would be out of danger and Michael wouldn't have to worry about her anymore.

Even though she didn't think anything would be missing from where she had hidden the jewels, Flanna decided to check on the treasure. She flipped up the area rug at the side of her worktable to reveal the pegged wooden floor beneath. Getting on her hands and knees, she poked at the loose board there until she could get a corner, then lifted it up.

The hollow beneath made a perfect hiding place. The squeak when she'd first stepped on it had given the loose board away.

Reaching inside, she scooped up the velvet-lined tray that

held a headpiece and bracelets and rings, set them on the floor next to her and for a moment admired her own handiwork. Replica and original cabochons held the same mesmerizing red fire. If she narrowed her gaze and looked deep into the authentic fire opals, Flanna imagined she could see Caillech burning at the stake.

Shuddering, she tried to shake off the weird sensation suddenly filling her, but couldn't. Her skin crawled, and feeling as if she were being watched, she nervously checked the dark corners of the room.

Nothing stared back.

And yet…

A quick glimpse at the window had her heart pounding. Had she really seen a shadow?

Scrambling to her feet, she ran to the glass and looked out. For a moment, all was still. Then a flurry of movement made her pulse jag. A bird flew upward.

It was only a bird.

Taking a deep breath, she muttered, "Idiot, what did you expect to see?" Then she returned to the jewelry, replacing the pieces on the tray with a shaky hand.

She set the tray back into its hidey-hole and heard a soft *clink*. One of the rings had simply come loose from its perch all the way in the back. Not wanting to deal with the tray again now to secure the piece—nerves were making her hands tremble—she would simply be careful when she retrieved the jewelry for Barry Rafferty the next day.

In the meantime, she set the pegged board back in place and re-covered it with the edge of the rug.

The itchy feeling still hadn't left her, but a second check of the room and gardens outside put her logical mind to rest.

Suddenly exhaustion caught up with her. Flanna changed

into a pair of cropped pants and a loose, frilly blouse and threw herself across the bed. On the nightstand, she'd placed framed family photographs. Keelin and Curran with their spouses and kids, her ma and da, and last but not least, her beloved gran.

Picking up the treasured remembrance, she lay on her back and looked into the kind eyes of the grandmother who'd lived for her family. She touched the face and felt both sentimental and sad.

"Ah, Gran, why couldn't you have lived forever?"

As always she thought of her grandmother's legacy to her nine grandchildren. She didn't need the letter, which she'd tucked away in a scrapbook back in Dublin. She'd read it so many times she could see it in her mind's eye.

To my darling Flanna,
I leave you my love and more. Within thirty-three days of your thirty-third birthday—enough time to know what you are about—you will have in your grasp a legacy of which your dreams are made. Dreams are not always tangible things, but more often are born in the heart. Act selflessly in another's behalf, and my legacy will be yours.

Your loving grandmother,
Moira McKenna
P.S. Use any other inheritance from me wisely and only for good, lest you destroy yourself or those you love.

Too bad she didn't believe in the spirit of the legacy. Oh, she believed in the "other inheritance" part. Sometimes she felt as if she'd spent her life either defending or hiding her gift. It was the promise of love that left her cold inside.

Erin Cassidy had seen to that.

Ever since that horrible day when she'd discovered how he'd been using her, how he'd made her an accomplice in his thieving scheme without her even suspecting, Flanna had made sure to protect her heart. She'd avoided involvement, had concentrated on her work.

And anytime an attractive man tempted her, she'd made sure he knew the truth about her gift and then had waited to see what he would do with that knowledge. Who would have guessed the truth could be the most effective form of birth control? She hadn't been with a man since Erin.

"You told me to wait, that if I was patient, the right man would come along," she whispered to Gran's photograph. "Too bad you were wrong."

MICHAEL HAD GIVEN the area around the cottage a once-over and had driven completely around the property before leaving for Garrity's pub. He still wasn't convinced they hadn't been followed from Rafferty Manor, nor was he certain the other vehicle hadn't tried running them off the road. But there was no dark vehicle lurking behind a hedgerow.

Relaxing a little, as much as he could considering the circumstances, Michael headed back to town. He hadn't wanted to leave Flanna alone, but he couldn't have her with him, not when he didn't know how Sean Hogan was going to react to his questioning.

An innocent like Flanna—and he was certain she was an innocent—would no doubt be horrified if he'd revealed how he was so familiar with the criminal mind. It was an explanation best left unspoken. She didn't need to know his history, he thought, even as something in him wondered how she would react if he told her about his past.

Would she run from him?

Or would she judge him by who and what he was now, what he had made of himself against the odds?

And why did it matter?

He had to stop thinking about it, stop obsessing over a woman who lived in a world far different than his own. His was a world of reality, hers one of fantasy. While fantasy could be charming, it simply wasn't real.

Garrity's pub was in the center of town. He had to search for a parking spot and walk back two blocks to the popular watering hole. The sun hadn't even set yet, but the pub was crowded.

A seat at the bar gave him a good view of the whole place. After ordering a dark beer, he checked out the bartender, a young guy with sandy hair and an open expression. One of the barmaids called him Owen.

"Is it always this crowded so early?"

"Aye, most nights. This place is the heart of Killarra. It's the longest-running business, that's for certain."

"That means you must know everyone in town."

"A fair assessment. Most everyone, anyway. All the long-timers."

"What about a guy named Sean Hogan?"

"What about him?" Owen asked, his smile fading a bit.

"Does he come in here often?"

"Often enough."

"Is he here now?" Michael casually ran his gaze around the place. "A friend asked me to say hello."

"A friend in America?"

"A friend from Cork." He picked a place without thinking, then realized Flanna's parents lived near Cork. "No big deal. He just said since I was coming here…"

"Sean's not here yet."

"Would you mind pointing him out if he does show?"

"Sure enough."

"Thanks," Michael said, tipping Owen an extra ten euros.

He drank slowly, took in the Irish accents all around him and shook his head at the rap on the jukebox. Where was the Irish music? He made the beer last nearly half an hour. A few men left and a few more came in, but no notice came from the bartender. Thinking it was true that a man only rented a beer, he made for the toilet. And when he came back out a few minutes later, he saw Owen talking intently with Eamon Rafferty and a dark-haired stranger. The conversation seemed furtive.

What were they so focused on? Michael wondered. And who was the second man?

He'd always trusted his instincts and when the stranger nodded to Eamon, slapped Owen's arm and started for the door, instinct made Michael believe he'd found Sean Hogan.

He waited until the man had the door open and was halfway out before following. He didn't need a confrontation with so many witnesses. Hogan was the local and no doubt many of the pub's patrons, along with the bartender, were his friends. Including Eamon Rafferty, just as Lisa had said.

Michael was soon out the door and seconds behind him. His surroundings were camouflaged by the flat light of dusk.

He swept his gaze over the street. No movement. Had his quarry really disappeared so quickly?

Then he spotted an irregularity in the doorway of a nearby shop. Someone stood there perfectly still.

Pulse thrumming, Michael moved in that direction, keeping his pace casual, his attention seemingly wandering to take in the sights around him. All the while, he was aware of the man standing still in the doorway. Watching him. Waiting for him to pass.

Michael took one step beyond the man, then stopped to face him. "Sean Hogan, I presume."

An explosion of movement sent Michael reeling backward as Hogan erupted out of the doorway. As fit as he was, he regained his balance quickly and was off after Hogan, who was running down the street like a man bent on avoiding trouble.

Michael quickly narrowed the gap between them and yelled, "Hogan, I just want to ask you a few questions."

"Go to hell!"

"Right behind you."

Michael sped up enough to close the distance between them. He tackled Hogan, sent them both crashing against a parked vehicle. Hogan slashed out with a fist. Michael ducked, spun the other man around so his back was against the car, and used a trigger point to cause him some pain. Hogan thrashed but wasn't able to free himself of the pressure.

"Just cool your jets and I'll let go. Simple as that. I just want to talk to you."

Hogan stopped struggling. "All right. So talk."

Michael let up the pressure but didn't move his hand away. "I've been told you might know something about the robbery that got Bridget Rafferty killed."

"Whoever told you that is a liar."

"But you are friends with her son Eamon, right?"

"Yeah, Eamon's my mate. We went through school together. So what?"

"How close are you?"

"What does that have to do with anything?"

"Close enough that he would tell you where to find a key to the house?"

"Bugger off!"

Hogan tried to push away and Michael reapplied pressure to the trigger point.

"I heard you set him up with a loan shark. Something in it for you?" When Hogan didn't answer, Michael said, "If you were working for someone else involved in the robbery and murder, now's the time to talk. It'll go easier on you."

"I don't know what you want from me! I had nothing to do with his mam's death. Or the bloody robbery. If you don't believe me, I can give you half a dozen names of blokes who can tell you I was cleaning them out at poker the night of the murder. Or you could just ask Detective Garda Kevin Murphy. He already checked me out."

Michael let go. "I'll do that."

Instinct and experience told him Hogan was telling the truth, at least about having an alibi. But alibis could be bought.

"If you know *anything*—"

"I don't!"

"Anything related to the crime and don't come clean about it, that makes you an accessory."

"Well, you'd have to prove that first, wouldn't you." Hogan grinned as if Michael's intensity amused him. "And what business is it of yours, anyway? You're not from here. These aren't your people."

"No one should get away with murder," Michael said, his voice cold. "Ever. I'm here to even the odds so that won't happen this time."

"Good luck to you, then. Just leave me out of it." Straightening his shirt, Hogan moved off. "I done my time."

Probably not enough.

Michael knew most crimes went undiscovered, unsolved or unpunished. Several of his old Irish gang buddies who ran numbers and protection for small businesses in Boston had never been convicted.

Not that he'd ever seen the inside of a jail cell himself.

Heading back for Garrity's pub, Michael decided to invest in one more beer and some socializing with the locals to see what the word on the street might be concerning Bridget Rafferty's murder.

TINKLING GLASS awoke her. Flanna opened her eyes to the semidarkened room. She'd fallen asleep on the bed, her hand on her gran's photo.

She must have been dreaming. Looking to the clock, she saw she'd been asleep for quite a while. As she replaced the photo on the nightstand, what sounded like a light thud from the other room froze her to the spot.

Her pulse fluttered and her breath caught in her throat as she listened hard. For a moment, she heard nothing. And then, just as she started to relax, started to move, a distinct *thunk* made her heart race like mad.

Someone was in the house.

In the next room.

She had to get out.

Knowing the only bedroom window stuck so it wouldn't open farther than a foot, Flanna realized her only escape was through the living area. She would have to pass by whomever had broken in.

Heart thudding so loud she thought the thief might be able to hear, she silently slid along the wall toward the door. Now she could clearly hear furtive but steady activity coming from her work area. She was closer to the front door than was the thief, who was working by flashlight. An occasional beam strayed toward the doorway.

When she recognized the sound of the floorboard being popped up, she peered out to see a dark silhouette bent over her supposedly secret hiding place and knew this was it. She had to make her move.

Eyes on the bent figure, she slid out of the bedroom and toward the front door. Only when she was halfway there, mentally going over the locks she'd have to open to get out, did she turn her back on the thief.

Handling the lock and doorknob with care, she dared to breathe…until the thief grabbed her from behind and pulled her from the door. She tried to turn and fight, but rough hands circled her neck, squeezing the fight out of her…until blackness descended.

Chapter Six

"Flanna…Flanna, wake up…."

The familiar male voice came to her from a distance, as if in a dream. Her mind in a fog, Flanna felt trapped and had to fight her way up to the urgent tone.

"C'mon, wake up. Open those beautiful green eyes. Be okay."

Flanna groaned and pried open her eyes to see Michael's gorgeous blue ones close to hers. All of him was close—too close for comfort. His arms encircled her and smashed her against his chest.

"Wh-what happened?" she croaked, her neck muscles feeling strained and sore.

"I just got back from Garrity's pub. The door was open, and you were here on the floor."

"The jewelry…"

She tried to sit up but Michael kept her from doing so.

"Not so fast. Take it easy. You were unconscious. You could have a concussion."

"He didn't hit me." Flanna motioned to her throat. Her voice was just a bit hoarse as she spoke. "He cut off my air until I blacked out…couldn't be gone long…" She tried to sit again to no avail.

"But he is gone. And thank God you're all right, though a doctor should look at that neck."

He was looking. And exploring with gentle fingers. Despite the situation, a thrill shot through her.

"How badly does it hurt?"

Her neck twinged a little. And then simply felt delicious. "Not bad," she choked out.

An unfamiliar languor spread through Flanna, and she settled back in Michael's arms for a moment. He seemed so concerned...so warm...so very attractive. Irresistible, really. She reached up and touched his face in return. He immediately froze and choked back a sound that didn't stop her exploration. She swept her fingertips along his beard-stubbled jawline to his chin and then to the curve of his bottom lip.

With a soft groan, Michael moved his face closer and took a fingertip in his mouth. His gentle sucking on the pad kick-started her pulse. Suddenly she found it difficult to breathe, to break visual contact with those mesmerizing blue eyes.

And then they were coming even closer.

His mouth covered hers. Softly. Sweetly. Made her heart thud. He nudged her lips and she opened gladly to his exploration. Her head went light and the rest of her quickened, and the next thing she knew, her arms wound around his neck, locking her to him.

The nature of the kiss changed, grew more demanding, subtly at first, then more insistent.

Part of her—the wild, reckless part that had gotten involved with Erin—responded and wanted more.

But the other part—the part that still remembered how cruelly Erin had betrayed her—put the brakes on her frustrated libido.

Her two halves struggled for control. The part that was

sensible and logical and yes, still angry after nearly five years, won.

Flattening a hand on Michael's chest, Flanna regretfully pushed him away.

For a moment, their gazes locked once more. They were both breathing heavily but now, rather than being warm and inviting, his eyes seemed distant. Cool. The rest of him followed as he pulled away both physically and emotionally.

"Sorry. That shouldn't have happened."

"No, it shouldn't have."

She should be sorry, too, but she couldn't quite get there. Embarrassed, she freed herself and sat up.

"Are you all right?" he asked.

"I could use some water."

"I'll get you a glass. And call the local police. And a doctor."

"No doctor. I'm fine."

Other than some soreness where the thief's fingers had pressed in to her throat, she really was.

With Michael in the kitchen, Flanna had room to breathe, to question her judgment and her attraction to the man least likely to meet any of her expectations. Not that she needed a man. She'd decided that long ago, despite her grandmother's legacy.

So why now?

Why him?

Dreams are not always tangible things, but more often are born in the heart. Act selflessly in another's behalf, and my legacy will be yours.

Could it be that her determination to find a thief and a killer, to reap justice for Bridget despite putting herself at risk, had changed the course of her life?

The idea was too scary, something she would rather not take out and examine now. Maybe later.

Maybe after things were settled and her life was back to normal.

After Michael had gone back to his America.

She could hear the murmur of Michael's voice as he talked on his cell over the sound of running water. The timbre of his voice stirred her, but she shook off the strange feeling. If there was ever a wrong time to get involved with someone, and a wrong man, this was it.

Quickly reorienting herself, Flanna got up and moved to the still-open section of flooring and looked down into the dark cavity. Could she get an impression of the thief? Thinking to try, she lowered her hand inside the hidey-hole, touched the tray that was still inside and concentrated.

Nothing.

She reached deeper and her fingers nicked something loose.

Her heart tumbled along with the ring that had dropped off the velvet-covered tray. She curled her fingers around the metal and pulled the ring from the hiding place.

Was it the original or the replica?

She closed her eyes for a moment and concentrated, and within a heartbeat saw a flash of red skirts and heard the rhythmic tap of cleated heels on floorboards.

The original.

Thankfully, the thief had missed it. The criminal collector was still short one piece of the Celtic suite.

Coming back from the kitchen, Michael said, "Detective Garda Murphy is on his way with a forensic team."

Palming the ring so he couldn't see it, Flanna nodded. "Good."

As if just realizing she'd moved, he asked, "What are you doing over here and still on the floor? Let me help you to your feet."

After furtively slipping the ring in her pocket, Flanna gave Michael her hand and let him pull her up. She was certain if she told him about it, he would make her give it up. She needed to think on the situation first. Instinct told her the ring might hold answers, ones only she could retrieve from it. But would it be worth the risk?

"Wait, what's that?" Near the discarded floorboard, Flanna suddenly spotted a piece of cloth that she'd never seen before.

"Looks like a scarf or a neck kerchief," Michael said. When she went for it, he added, "Don't pick it up."

She already had it in her hand.

Her head went light and the room narrowed....

A fist wrapped in the cloth punched through a window. Glass shattered and a calloused hand undid the lock.

"Flanna, what's going on?"

Ignoring Michael, Flanna focused on the thief and his break-in.

No dark gloves like last time. Her focus traveled up a forearm sprinkled with dark hair to a tribal tattoo circling the muscular upper arm. A Celtic knot with a horse's head in the center.

"Flanna, what's wrong?"

This time Michael touched her and she came right out of the trance and swayed. Before she could catch herself, he slid one arm under her legs, the other around her back, and carried her to the couch.

"I'm fine," she protested, even as the room swam around her.

"Good," he said, setting her down. "But stay put anyway, until we're sure."

"I had another vision," she said, then was interrupted by the siren announcing the arrival of the *gardai*.

THOUGH THE POLICE went over the room painstakingly, they found nothing more significant than the piece of cloth that Flanna had mistakenly touched. Ruggedly middle-aged with worry lines etched across his seamed face and up into his receding hairline, Detective Garda Kevin Murphy interviewed both of them and appeared frustrated that he was getting pretty much nowhere.

Thankfully, she wasn't trying to convince Murphy that she'd supposedly had some psychic vision, Michael thought. No doubt she kept that story to herself because she knew the detective would see right through her.

"I don't ken there's anything else we can do now," Murphy said. "The boyos will check those fingerprints they're getting now against the two of yours. If there's no match, then we might have something to go on."

"I hope so," Michael said.

He'd met Murphy when he'd arrived in Killarra. The detective hadn't been enthusiastic about his investigation, even though Michael had an intro from Interpol.

"I still don't understand what happened at the Rafferty crime site. No trace evidence." Murphy shook his head. "At least we got something here."

"Wait. Did you say no trace evidence?" Michael asked. "My case in Boston was the same." He wondered if that had been true of the London theft/murder, as well.

"Peculiar, it is. A very fastidious criminal."

"Or one who knows how to use magic to obliterate any evidence," Flanna murmured.

Murphy gave Flanna a wary look but didn't respond to her comment. "If you remember anything else—"

"Murphy," Michael interrupted, "you might want to look in to Sean Hogan's alibi."

"Sean Hogan. How is it you know our local bad boy?"

"In case you weren't aware of it, he's a friend of Eamon Rafferty's. I was told he found a loan shark to help Eamon out of trouble recently. I wondered about his access to Rafferty Manor—not that he admitted anything, of course. He denies knowing anything about the robbery or the murder."

"You spoke to him when?"

"Earlier today. Right before the robbery, as a matter of fact. Then I went back into Garrity's pub to see if anyone had good information."

"And?"

"Nothing there, either, unfortunately. My instincts are good, though, and I would bet Hogan knows something if he wasn't directly involved. My going back into the pub gave him enough time for him to come here with Flanna alone and finish what he started."

"It wasn't him," Flanna said of Hogan.

"How can you be sure of that?" Murphy asked. "I thought you didn't see the thief's face."

"I didn't. I don't even know what Sean Hogan looks like."

"Then how can you be certain it wasn't him?"

"I—I just know."

"Ah, so 'tis like that, is it?" Murphy said. "Barry Rafferty warned me about you, Flanna McKenna. Said you fancy yourself some kind of a psychic."

"I don't fancy myself anything."

"When we need the services of someone in touch with other worlds, I'll be letting you know first thing."

"You do that," Flanna said irritably.

Suddenly the door banged open and Barry Rafferty himself strutted in, and said, "I heard there was trouble here."

"Indeed there was," Murphy said. "A robbery. You're trampling over a crime site."

"Only to get what's mine." Barry zeroed in on Flanna. "I came to get my mother's jewelry."

"Didn't you hear the detective?" Michael asked. "There's been a *robbery*."

Flanna added, "You'll have to wait until the thief is caught to get both the originals and replicas."

"What?" Barry's face turned a dark red. "You're saying it's all gone? You just turned over something of such value to a criminal?"

"I turned nothing over to no one."

"Flanna was attacked," Michael said. "You should be thankful she's all right."

"She was careless. She should have turned over everything upon learning of my mother's death! I asked you directly for the pieces yesterday!"

"And if you had been able to pay me, I would have given them to you right off."

"You'll not be paid for anything now. And you look all right to me." Barry was practically spitting as he spoke. He turned to Murphy. "It's too convenient that when we demand what rightfully belongs to the Raffertys, it disappears. I demand you arrest this woman as an accomplice!"

"There'll be no arrests made tonight, not of Flanna McKenna."

Barry's face reddened. His expression vicious, he turned on Flanna. "I'll—I'll ruin you for this! You'll never get work again!" he spat, before wheeling around and marching back out the door.

"I wouldn't cross that one." Murphy shook his head and waved to his men, who seemed to be finished with the scene, to indicate they should leave. "If you remember anything—"

"We'll let you know," Michael promised. He waited only until the *gardai* were out the door before turning back to Flanna. "So why are you so certain Hogan isn't the one who attacked you? Does it have something to do with this vision you announced before Murphy arrived?"

She had been acting weirdly when he'd come out of the kitchen, but it undoubtedly had been the result of the attack on her.

"I'm afraid it does."

Michael clenched and unclenched his jaw. "What did you supposedly see that has you so certain?"

"A tattoo. When I picked up the scarf, I saw the thief breaking through the window. He wasn't wearing gloves like the vision about Bridget's murder. He used the scarf to cover his hand to break the glass. His sleeves were short, so I could see his upper arm and the tribal tattoo that encircled it."

Thinking that she was confused by the stressful situation, that she'd probably gotten a quick look at the guy's arm before he'd squeezed the air from her throat, Michael asked, "What does the tattoo have to do with anything?"

"It was a Celtic knot with a horse's head in the middle. I've seen that tattoo before."

"You know the guy?"

"Not exactly. I'm familiar with the ethnic group he's part of. Irish Travelers. A specific clan that maintain their connection to horses."

"You mean the gypsies who travel in horse-drawn caravans?"

"They're not really gypsies. They are of Irish origin in fact. An ethnic group. They're people who aren't what we call settled," she explained. "And not all of the caravans are horse-drawn anymore, either. Many Travelers have modernized. For some who want to keep tradition alive, the horse's head tattoo is a reminder of their roots. Some of them still have kept their horse-drawn caravans, while others own horses or are in the horse trade."

She sounded very convincing. Perhaps she believed everything she was saying. That didn't mean that *he* did.

"Why didn't you tell all this to Murphy?"

"Do you think he would have believed I had a peek into the past?"

"Do you think *I* do?"

A sound of exasperation passed her bowed lips. Lips that he had now tasted. How in the hell had he let that happen? Flanna McKenna was tempting, too tempting for his peace of mind. He needed to keep things on a professional level between them. Part of him wanted to walk away from her, find someone sane to help him, but she had been working on the jewelry. He didn't know who could be of more help.

She said, "I'm going to find him."

"What?"

"I'm going to find the man who broke in here."

"How?"

"With this." She dug in her pocket and when she pulled her hand out, she turned it over and opened it.

"A ring? That's the copy you made, right?"

She shook her head. "'Tis the original."

Michael stared at Flanna. He hadn't thought she had it in her to be dishonest. He'd convinced himself she was innocent. What did she think she was doing keeping the ring? And then showing it to him, of all people?

"You have the ring and didn't tell Murphy? Or turn it

over to Barry Rafferty when he asked for it? So you're a liar and a thief."

A flicker of pain crossed her features, and when she gazed at him, her eyes looked glassy, as if she were trying to keep herself from crying.

"No untruth passed my lips. And I don't mean to keep the ring, just to have it in my possession awhile longer. The Raffertys haven't paid me yet, either, so I'm in my rights to hold on to this until I am."

"They think all the pieces were stolen."

"Did I say any such thing?"

Thinking back, he realized she'd phrased her answers so she hadn't had to lie. "No, but—"

"Well, then."

Michael raked a hand through his hair. "What if you can get your payment tomorrow? Would that make a difference? Would you then admit you have the original ring and turn it over?"

"I need the ring with me," Flanna argued. "Thankfully, he didn't get the ring, or the killer would have the entire suite and with Beltane less than a week away. You have no idea what someone with Caillech's powers could do."

Powers? Did an intelligent woman really believe such superstition? Michael knew his expression was one of disbelief when Flanna averted her gaze.

"I'm hoping the ring will help me find its mates and therefore the thief," she said.

"How?" And then he realized what she was getting at. "Supernaturally?"

She nodded.

"Bah!"

The explosive negation left him before he could so much

as think to be a little more tactful. He couldn't help it. How gullible did she think he was?

Her expression neutral, she said, "You must do what you think is best for the case, of course, while I do the same. It's a matter of honor that I find the pieces that were entrusted to me. And to stop anyone else from dying over them. The jewelry is part of Bridget's estate and I couldn't just hand over the ring to her wastrel son, who might be guilty of seeing his own mother dead. I need to find the truth. It's my way of honoring the dead."

Michael thought Flanna believed what she was saying. All of it. Perhaps she was simply a bit touched which would make her more vulnerable to any wrongdoers.

With a sense of resignation, he asked, "What is it you're planning?"

"To find the Traveler who broke in here tonight and learn the truth from him."

"You'll get yourself killed!"

"Not if I'm careful."

"You said you could handle being alone while I spoke to Sean Hogan and look what happened to you!"

She ignored him. "There's not much time. If the killer manages to get this ring from me…I need to do what I need to do."

"Not without me."

"What?"

Her eyes widened in surprise, and Michael felt himself falling into them again. No, he couldn't go there. Neither could he leave Flanna to work on her own.

"You need protection until this case is resolved." He was already angry with himself for not protecting Flanna earlier as he knew he should have. "I'll go with you tomorrow. Tonight I stay here. You're not leaving my sight again."

"You think I'll flee in the middle of the night?"

"If the thief realizes he doesn't have the original ring, he might come back for it."

When she said, "I only have one bed," he grinned at her. And then she took away the pleasure as quickly as she'd instilled it. "And a couch. You can sleep on that."

Michael bit the inside of his mouth to keep from groaning. The fragile, frilly thing would hardly accommodate his big frame. But he wasn't going anywhere. And it had nothing to do with his attraction to her. Following up on that kiss would be unprofessional. If he allowed Flanna to distract him, he might as well give up now.

He had to concentrate on his reason for being thousands of miles from home.

He had jewelry to find, not to mention a murderer. Everything in him had to be focused on bringing the killer to justice.

He couldn't stand to let a murderer go free when he could make sure that didn't happen.

Not again.

Chapter Seven

After a nearly sleepless night tossing and turning, thinking of Michael in the next room, Flanna woke at dawn having had little rest. Even now, he was the first thought in her head. Thinking about being with him in a more physical way was tempting. Too tempting. She hadn't been with a man since Erin. No man had moved her or seemed so attractive…not until Michael Eagan.

What had she been thinking of, going and kissing him, for heaven's sake? And, oh, what a kiss, one that had kept her awake wondering…

She needed to stop this, to get herself under control.

She needed a shower.

Wrapping herself in a fluffy long robe, Flanna cautiously opened the door and peered out. Soft snoring came from the direction of the couch, so she supposed it was safe enough to get to the bathroom unnoticed. She could have her shower and be dressed before Michael so much as opened an eye.

Silently crossing to the bathroom door, Flanna mistakenly glanced over to where he slept. An expanse of uncovered male flesh mesmerized her. The sheet covered him from hips to knees and pooled at the foot of the couch. His chest was broad and smooth and narrowed to a tight, muscular abdomen, making her long to see what lay below.

Telling herself to breathe, she escaped into the bathroom and into the shower where she let a stream of water pound some sense into her, not just about Michael, but about her plan.

Was she doing the right thing?

Having no training in this sort of investigation, perhaps she should leave it to the authorities and offer her help.

Then again, Detective Garda Murphy was of a mind to make light of her gift. He would never see it as being in his best interests to accept her help. Even if he did, he might not believe her visions, might not let her get close enough to have them.

On the other hand, though she might be a novice, Michael was a trained investigator. Thank the stars he'd insisted on accompanying her.

Flanna had some deep-seated need to find the jewelry that had been entrusted to her. Even more important, she had to stop the deaths and put an end to the curse. How she was going to manage such a feat, Flanna didn't know. Assuming she and Michael were able to retrieve the collection, they would still have to convince the disbelieving and greedy Raffertys to honor their mother's wishes. She doubted Bridget had amended her will to include Caillech's jewelry, since she'd meant to donate the originals to the museum herself as soon as the replicas were finished.

Flanna had taken just a bit too much time. Perhaps if she'd finished a day earlier...

But she hadn't.

And now she had to live with that whisper of guilt in the best way she knew how. She had to fix things.

One thing at a time.

First she had to find the man who'd robbed her.

MICHAEL WOKE and tried focusing on his pocket watch, the cracked face adding to the difficulty. Bleary-eyed, he realized it was nearly 8:00 a.m.

"I'm up!" he announced.

"Jump in the shower, then, while I'm getting food on the table."

"I'll be done in a flash!"

Michael stumbled to his feet, wrapping the sheet around him. The couch had been too cramped, too hot. He'd been able to deal with the heat by stripping, but he hadn't been able to take the couch any longer. He was stiff and sore and had difficulty standing up straight.

The shower helped. Hot water soothed his body and cleared his head. Then he pulled on fresh jeans and a cotton shirt, and rolled the sleeves to the elbows, but decided a shave could wait.

His need for coffee couldn't.

The kitchen was only a few steps away. Unfortunately, there was no coffee in sight.

"Have a cuppa," Flanna said, handing him a steaming mug.

"What is this?"

"Tea, of course."

"Uh, thanks." He took a slug and wondered how he was going to function. "Did you call your landlord about the broken window?" He'd put a board in front of it before going to bed, but he hadn't the tools to do a proper job.

"I did. He'll take care of it this morning."

"Good," he said, as she set two plates on the table. Both were piled with eggs and grilled tomato and sausages—a real Irish breakfast. Sitting, he asked, "You can eat all that?"

"I'm starving. I don't remember eating yesterday other than some brown bread and jam with tea last night."

Michael suppressed a twinge of guilt. He'd gotten himself a hearty meal at the pub. "Looks and smells great."

"Eat up, then."

As Michael ate, he studied Flanna. She appeared delicate, yet demolished her breakfast like a lumberjack. Only one of many surprises about her. He suspected getting to know her better would reveal a lot more.

He already knew she was strong-willed and had a complex sense of honor. That she hadn't given up the ring bothered him, and yet part of him understood why—she really seemed to think it would help her find the thief. Believing in fairy tales might be a charming trait, but in this instance, her notion that the curse was real and that the ring could help her find its mates was misplaced.

"So how do you propose to start your search?" he asked.

"I know of a few legal Travelers' sites in the area. We'll start with the closest."

"There are illegal sites?"

"'Tis illegal to camp on the side of the highway or on settled land without permission. Some still do anyway despite the posted signs because there aren't enough established sites for all the Traveler families. Even though some of them now live in the same site for years, others in cities or towns in houses, they don't want to be considered settled themselves. They want to honor their heritage and do so by occasionally traveling around the countryside before coming back to their more permanent homes. They believe no one can really own the land and it should be available to all."

"In my country, Native Americans believe the same. Or used to. Many tribes were once nomadic, as well. Now they also have camps of a sort, only we call them reservations."

"Quite a difference between the land on a reservation and

a piece of tarmac for trailers run by a civil servant who goes to his own home every night. There are people everywhere in the world who want to live simple lives. Not everyone is in love with technology. I suppose anyone who is different gets grief of some sort from others. People always disagree with something other people believe in."

Wondering if she included herself in the *different* group, Michael said, "Disagreements drive the world."

"Or they destroy it. Just think what the world might be like without conflict."

Michael figured Flanna was thinking of the religious troubles that divided Ireland, but she quickly turned the conversation to a lighter topic until they finished eating. Still, he'd gotten a glimpse into her psyche. Not only was she a talented jewelry designer, as evidenced by the pounded bronze collar and matching cuffs on both wrists she wore today, but she was intelligent and compassionate—both traits to be admired.

Feeling a bit closer to Flanna, Michael enjoyed just being near her as he helped her clear the dishes and wipe down the table before they set out for the day.

"I'll drive, you navigate," he said, opening the passenger door to the Renault.

A good drive took them to a clearing in the woods a short distance from another town. Nearly a dozen R.V.s or trailers stood scattered in a circle, a few of the last with trucks that hauled them still attached. One truck sat yards from a trailer. Another trailer sat alone as if its owner had driven off and abandoned it.

At one end of the camp, a pile of scrap metal made a small mountain. In the center, dozens of kids played in the dirt, while adults in chairs under awnings or trees watched on. One woman had managed to do her laundry and was hanging wet clothes on a line strung from her trailer to the nearest tree branch. And a man was stacking chopped wood by what seemed to be a communal fire.

When the Renault pulled up to the camp and stopped, all activity and conversation ceased. Michael realized Flanna had pulled out the ring and was studying it intently.

"See something that'll lead us to the rest of the suite?" he asked.

"No, nothing."

She flushed and dropped it back into a pouch, which she then shoved into a pocket.

Michael felt all eyes on him and Flanna as they got out of the car. Thinking his American accent would put off the Travelers, he murmured, "You take the lead."

Flanna nodded. "A good day to you all!" She looked around with a friendly smile.

One little kid smiled back and seemed about to say something when an older girl pulled him back, closer to their trailer.

"Is anyone here in charge of the camp?"

"This is a legal site."

A rough-hewn red-haired man stood from a wood-and-cloth director's chair. He wasn't tall, but he was brawny. And he had attitude, Michael thought, as he pulled close to Flanna to give her backup.

"I'm not from the government," Flanna assured him. "I'm simply looking for someone. It would be grand if I could ask you a few questions."

The leader sat and waved them over. "Ask away."

As they crossed the small field, Michael noticed the parents corralled their kids protectively and watched from the shade of their respective trailers. The families were large; a few couples were surrounded by as many as seven or eight kids. Most eyes were on *him,* most expressions were tight, as if he represented a threat to them.

Still smiling as they got close to the leader, Flanna said, "My name is Flanna McKenna, and I'm looking for a Traveler, a man—"

"His name?" The leader didn't offer his own.

"I wouldn't be knowing that. What I do know is that a tattoo circles his upper right arm—a Celtic knot with a horse's head."

The leader nodded as if he knew exactly what she was talking about. "Many members of the horsemen clan wear the stallion's head."

She'd heard of the clan though she'd never met one of them until she'd been attacked. "In this area?"

"They come and go."

"In caravans or trailers?"

The leader leaned back in his chair and carefully scrutinized Flanna. "You're awfully curious about one of us for a non-Pavee. Why do you seek this man?"

"He may have information I need."

"I'm sorry I can't help."

"You can't tell me where I can find anyone with such a tattoo?"

"We don't give out that kind of information even if we had it."

That was it, then, the end of the conversation. The man rose, turned his back on them and walked into his trailer.

Her expression one of frustration, Flanna shrugged. "We might as well go, then." She looked around. "None of these people are going to speak to us."

As was the case in the next two camps they visited. The day was gone before they knew it.

"We might as well go back, then," Michael said as he headed the car toward Killarra. "This is getting us nowhere. Apparently no Traveler is going to give an outsider information about one of their own."

The day had been a bust, but he wasn't sure what he could have done to yield better results. Talking to more of the townspeople wouldn't do them any good if the thief truly was a Traveler. And while he didn't believe in Flanna's visions, he was certain she had seen that tattoo on the man's arm before being knocked out. It was still the best lead they had.

"We'll have to start again in the morning, then," she said. "Go in a different direction."

Michael was amazed that Flanna didn't seem to get it. "You realize we probably won't be any more successful than we were today." Not without a plan. "We would just keep spinning our wheels."

"Then spin they must. I can't let this go, Michael. I can't let a killer walk free if there is anything I can do to bring him to justice."

Though he didn't think tomorrow would be any different, he didn't argue. He didn't have a plan. Yet.

But about bringing a killer to justice…he agreed with her completely.

WHAT IN THE HELL did the McKenna woman think she was about? Bad enough she'd forced a second robbery to get possession of the remaining pieces. Bad enough the American had been around, making things more difficult.

Now she seemed to be working with him, asking questions, putting her nose in places it didn't belong.

Time to neutralize…and to take care of another problem, as well.

"I have a job for you."

Sean Hogan smiled. "You know as long as money is involved, I'm open to anything."

"Good. Take this."

Hogan took the ring. The fire opal cabochon glowed as it caught the light. "You want me to fence this?"

The fool thought it was the real thing rather than a duplicate. The work was so good, it had been easily mistaken for the genuine article.

"I want you to hide it somewhere easily found in the McKenna woman's cottage. You can do that, can't you? Get in without anyone knowing?"

"No lock can hold me back," he agreed. "Getting in and out of places unseen is my specialty. But I don't get the point of giving this back to her."

"After you plant it, the *gardai* station will get an anonymous telephone call…."

Hogan's eyes widened and then his lips curved into a broad grin. He seemed both surprised and amused. "You're setting her up?"

Problem-solving was an art. "I'm getting her out of the way."

And him.

Killing two problem birds with one stone.

FLANNA FINISHED a cup of herbal tea meant to let her sleep well that night. Gran had kept an herbal garden and had shared her knowledge of medicinal plants with her granddaughters. Her sister, Keelin, having inherited the skill and the garden, was an herbalist. Flanna had caught on to a few of the basics, but she'd never taken them further. However, needing a good night's sleep, as did Michael, she'd brewed her grandmother's special recipe. Michael had taken a cup, as well—not that he believed in herbal remedies any more than he did anything else she told him having to do with her grandmother.

Even so, he was looking sleepy already.

That couch was really too small for Michael. If she wanted to be generous, she could offer him her bed and take the couch herself. For a moment she imagined him in her bed…in her arms…

Suddenly flushed with warmth, Flanna said, "Perhaps we should make plans for tomorrow."

She'd hoped the ring would be of some help, but she'd gotten nothing off it. Not so much as a weird feeling. Though she'd tried to look deeply into the fire opal, she'd seen nothing, not even the whirling skirts of the flamenco dancer. Perhaps she had to be in a different state of mind to read something from it. All she'd managed to do was increase Michael's certainty that there was nothing to her gift.

"Like I said before, no one is going to talk to us," Michael stated, "at least not if they think we're outsiders."

He sounded as if he had an idea. "Your point?"

"We can try going undercover."

"Undercover? You mean pretend we're Travelers?"

"Why not? We get a small trailer, a change of clothes and we're all set."

"Not really. You don't know their language. Gammon or Shelta is a language that uses not only Gaelic and English but made-up words. A language meant to keep Traveler secrets. I can barely understand it myself." Flanna had volunteered for a time helping Travelers in Dublin get social services, and so she'd picked up some, what they call the Cant, but that had been years ago. How much she could remember she didn't know. "They do speak English, but nothing is to say they might not switch. Then what?" Flanna couldn't suppress a yawn. "And there's your accent—"

"We can fake it. If you understand any of what they say, you can respond in English. And I can keep my mouth shut and play the taciturn husband."

Starting, Flanna blinked and tried to focus. The herbs had made her a bit bleary-eyed and she longed for her bed. "Husband?"

"Right. From what I saw, Travelers are all about family. Big families. We don't have kids, so we'll have to pose as newly-weds." As if he read her instant discomfort, Michael said, "We'll pose as a married couple in name only, of course. Nothing to worry about."

But she *was* worrying.

Newlyweds…a small trailer…cramped space…just the two of them…

Even without the idea as an incentive, she'd had licentious thoughts about the man. What would happen if they spent so much time together squeezed into cramped quarters?

Her pulse skittered through her as she asked, "Do you really think it could work?"

"What choice do we have?" Michael yawned and shook his head as if he were having trouble keeping his eyes open. "I don't know how else we can find the Traveler who broke in here. I doubt people play at being one of them, so they won't have reason to think we're anything but what we say we are. We simply have to hope we don't run in to anyone we've already met."

A little breathless, Flanna nodded. "All right. We'd better get some sleep, then."

Her bed summoned her with a siren's call.

"Good night." Michael was already settling himself on the couch. "We'll talk about it first thing in the morning."

Flanna nodded and headed for the bedroom.

Try as she might—and she did try—she couldn't think of a better plan.

THE PLAN WAS working perfectly.

Hogan's car pulled in at the hedgerow in the middle of the night. He got out, patted his pocket and made for the McKenna woman's cottage.

The fool didn't so much as look over his shoulder to see if anyone was watching. He seemed deaf, as if he didn't notice the start of another car engine.

Good.

Exactly as planned.

And exactly as he said, he easily got in to the cottage. He wasn't inside long. Only a few minutes passed and then he was out the door and crossing back to his own car.

The watcher edged the vehicle forward until Hogan was in the middle of the open area. Then gunned it. The vehicle jumped to life, headlights bright so when Hogan whirled around, he froze, caught like a deer.

Vehicle and human connected.

Hogan literally flew through the air and landed a few yards from the stoop.

With a squeal of tires, the vehicle left the area without ever being seen.

Chapter Eight

A loud thump and a screech of tires awakened Flanna.

At first, she thought she'd been dreaming. Then she realized she heard a vehicle racing off. Stumbling out of bed, she shoved bare feet into a pair of mules and then wrapped a blanket around her shoulders before leaving the bedroom.

Michael was already on his feet, dressed and heading for the front door.

"You heard it, too, then?" she asked.

"It sounded like a car hitting a deer."

But it wasn't a deer sprawled on the front lawn.

"Saints have mercy, a man's been hit."

"Not just any man," Michael said, already on his knees and feeling for a pulse. "It's Sean Hogan and he's dead."

The breath caught in Flanna's throat and her stomach knotted. Though she didn't know him, she said a silent prayer for the man's soul.

Only after she'd made the sign of the cross did she murmur, "What in the world was Sean Hogan doing here and in the middle of the night?"

"I was wondering that myself." Michael rolled up the man's sleeve. "No tattoo."

Flanna started. "You thought he was the thief come back for the missing ring?"

"It was a thought."

About to announce her intention to go inside and call the *garda* station, Flanna heard a thin wail cutting through the night. Turning to the sound, she saw headlights flashing through the trees. A white vehicle with yellow and blue stripes along the body and blue lights flipping overhead advanced on them and pulled over.

"The driver must have called it in," Flanna said.

Someone *had* made a telephone call, but it hadn't been about a hit-and-run, they soon learned from Detective Garda Murphy, who looked put out at being summoned in the middle of the night.

"What's going on here?"

"A hit-and-run," Michael said. "We were sleeping and heard the accident. The driver ran off."

Murphy gave them both an accusing look before stooping next to the body.

Flanna grasped the blanket tighter around her while the detective made certain Hogan had no pulse. After that he gave orders to one of his men to call out the support team, who would assess the site and the body.

Then he asked Michael and Flanna to step inside and gestured for another of his men to follow.

"What's this about?" Michael demanded.

"I have a warrant to search the premises." He held it out to Flanna, who stared at it as if it would bite her.

"For what?" She feared the answer before it came from Murphy's mouth.

"We've had a tip that we'll find a piece of the jewelry from

Bridget's collection in your cottage. A piece that you failed to turn over last night after the supposed theft."

Lord, had the thief decided to get revenge on her, as if it were her fault that he'd missed the ring?

"Supposed?" she echoed. "You saw the broken window! And the thief choked me until I passed out!"

"You didn't see a doctor about it."

"Because I was all right. Merely bruised."

"Then you should have no objection to the search."

"No, of course not."

But of course she did have an objection she could not voice—her fear that they would find the ring she hadn't turned over after the theft.

Panic in her heart, Flanna stepped back and bumped into Michael. She felt the solidness of his shoulder. His arm slipped around her back to give her support.

"Where did this tip come from?" Michael asked.

"An anonymous call."

"And you gave it credence?"

"The informant said you had made a deal with Sean Hogan. He said that Hogan was on his way here to provide you with an introduction to a fence for the piece and that you would share the profits with him."

"That's ridiculous!" Flanna said, registering the fact that the tipster had been a man. Eamon Rafferty, perhaps? Or had it been Barry?

Murphy looked from her to Michael. "Owen Ryan claims you were in Garrity's pub looking for Hogan Sunday evening."

"As part of my investigation," Michael said. "If you'll get your facts straight, that was before the robbery."

"Maybe you set that up, too."

"You're reaching, Murphy. This was some kind of setup.

You've been a cop long enough to tell the difference. If you'll remember I tried putting you on to Hogan in the first place. When we went to check out the noise outside, the front door was unlocked," Michael told him. "I think Hogan had been in here, but without our knowledge. I didn't see any gloves on his hands, so take prints in here, see if his match. And let's see…who could have done the setting up? A man, right? Did you know Hogan and Eamon are old friends? As a matter of fact, they came into Garrity's together."

"*Were* friends," Murphy said. "The man's dead, after all. Sean Hogan and Eamon Rafferty did grow up in the same small village, so they knew each other all their lives. It would have been curious if they'd never lifted a pint together. Them being acquainted and all isn't cause for suspicion. But the fact that we found Hogan dead outside with the two of you standing over him is a different story altogether."

Shocked that Murphy was suggesting they had something to do with Hogan's death, as well, Flanna watched him and the uniformed *garda* search the room, opening every drawer, looking in every nook and cranny. And when the *garda* entered her bedroom, her entire body broke out in a nervous sweat.

What if he found the ring? And if he did, how would she explain it?

Sweat trickled between Flanna's breasts. It would be bad enough if she was arrested. Much worse if Michael was held accountable when he had nothing to do with it other than to keep silent. She felt horrible. She gave him a stricken look, tried to convey how sorry she was that she'd gotten him into this mess.

As if he understood her perfectly and was trying to say they were in this together, Michael hugged her tightly to him. Flanna felt only a tiny bit better for it. Her guilt was not so easily assuaged.

Hearing more sirens, she looked outside as the support truck pulled up, followed by an ambulance.

Suddenly, Murphy called, "Larkin, I found it!"

Flanna whipped around to see the detective reach into an empty vase and pull out a ring. Her heart thudded. That wasn't right. She'd hidden the ring in the bedroom, so how did it get out here?

"Let me see that," she said, rushing to Murphy's side.

"Now why would I be handing this over to you?"

"Please, just let me have a look. You can shoot me if I try to escape with it."

Reluctantly, he handed the ring to her. The moment she connected with the ring, her head went light and the room went out of focus…

A hand in a dark glove shoved the ring at Hogan.

Hogan took the ring and turned it over to get a better look.

"You want me to fence this?"

"Flanna, what's going on?" Michael asked.

The vision interrupted, Flanna blinked at him but didn't answer. She forced her mind to go deeper….

"All right. I'll do as you say. Pity you don't want to fence it, though," Hogan said. "But then, you've agreed to give me what's coming to me, so what do I care?"

"I'll have the ring back now."

Knocked out of the vision for good this time, Flanna tried to focus on Murphy, but her sight was still skewed and her knees wobbly. Apparently impatient, he snatched the ring from her hand.

"Are you all right?" Michael asked.

Once again he was there to steady her. Once again, she depended on his strength.

"I'm fine," she assured him. "Just a little light-headed."

"As I imagine you would be since you've been caught red-handed," Murphy said.

Flanna shook her head. "That ring is the replica I made, not the original. And I swear I didn't put it in that vase. It was stolen from me yesterday. Hogan must have gotten in somehow and planted it before he was hit."

"And I'm to believe you, why?"

"You don't have to believe me about the ring. You can get an expert from the Hunt Museum in Limerick to confirm that this is, indeed, the replica. Ask for one of the curators of arts and antiquities—Neal Brown, if he's available."

"Even if it is a replica, it still is in your cottage when you reported it stolen."

"Technically, since she was never paid for her work, the replica belongs to Flanna," Michael said. "So there's nothing illegal about her having it. But she's right that Hogan must have planted it here."

"If I believed that…why?" Murphy asked. "What was his motive?"

"To make Flanna look guilty, to get attention away from him, I imagine."

While that sounded good, Flanna knew as well as Michael did that Hogan had not been the man who'd robbed her.

"We'll sort this out at the station," Murphy said grudgingly. "You can give us your full statement there."

"And you'll check on the authenticity of the ring, won't you?" Flanna asked.

The detective didn't answer, merely said, "You'd better get dressed unless you want to come down to the station in your nightclothes."

Flanna retreated to the bedroom and changed. She didn't dare check on the ring she *had* hidden.

She only hoped it would still be there when she returned.

DÉJÀ VU. Running his thumb over the crack in his watch's face, Michael wondered if his past had finally caught up with him. Would he pay for a crime he hadn't committed to make up for ones he had?

He'd been in rooms like this one before, but never because of something *he* had done. He'd visited his father, brother and uncle when they'd been brought in. They'd always gotten off without serving time, and young fool that he had been, he'd expected he would have the luck of the Irish, as well. He'd always assumed he would have an important role in the family business once he finished school. It had taken one tragic day—one minute to be exact—to change not only his way of thinking, but also his life's course.

Now here he was, so many years later, in a situation he couldn't even have imagined for himself. He'd thought the past was behind him.

Maybe he should hire an attorney right away, but that would delay their investigation. He decided to wait and see if Murphy would keep an open mind.

After taking their statement and asking hundreds of questions, the detective had agreed to bring the ring to the Hunt Museum in Limerick to determine whether it was the original or the replica. He'd left Michael and Flanna together in an interrogation room, which meant they needed to be careful about what they said.

Undoubtedly the walls had ears.

And eyes.

Flanna sat in the chair opposite him, her own eyes closed, her breathing even. She seemed to be asleep. A slight flush colored her cheeks, and her lips were soft and pink. A lovely sight. A woman he would like to get to know better despite her imaginings about some psychic gift. He wouldn't hold it against her. Actually, it was part of her charm. Too bad he had to keep a professional distance.

He did believe her about the ring. She'd shown him the original after the robbery, so it didn't make sense that she would have kept the copy and not told him about that one also…which meant Hogan had broken in to the cottage and planted it in the vase.

Michael damned himself for drinking that herbal tea. He should have known better than to let down his guard even for a minute. Even so, he should have awakened at the slightest disturbance. The bastard must really have been good to get past him.

But why had Hogan done it?

Had he come in to find the original? That would make sense if he were the thief, but he wasn't. No tattoo. Was he working hand-in-hand with the thief, maybe introducing the real thief to the fence? But why would he risk himself by breaking in to the cottage to plant a fake ring?

If Hogan had been aware it was fake.

And what about his death? A hit-and-run right after he planted the ring seemed too coincidental. At least Murphy couldn't pin that one on them. His men had found tire tracks. The prints didn't match those made by either his or Flanna's tires.

Suddenly Flanna sat with a start and rapidly blinked. "How long?"

"Murphy's been gone over an hour. Shouldn't be much longer. How are you doing?"

"I'm fine."

"I thought you were going to pass out on me back at the cottage."

"I always get a little dizzy after having one of my spells." Her expression was covert when she added, "Later."

So she didn't want to share her visions with any *garda* who might be listening. No big surprise. He wondered what she would say she saw this time.

Michael tried to make small talk but he could tell Flanna's heart wasn't in the exchange, so he let it be. Murphy returned soon enough, and Flanna jumped up.

"Well?"

"You were right. The ring I found is the replica."

"We've answered all your questions," Michael said, "and you got a confirmation on the ring. I assume we're free to go."

"For now, yes. I have nothing to establish a case against you. Yet."

"Listen to you, Murphy. Threatening one of the victims with arrest. You'd spend your time better going after the real criminal in this case."

Murphy didn't respond, merely held the interrogation door open for them.

Michael wasted no time in ushering Flanna through it and out of the station. It was after eleven and his empty stomach was protesting.

"We should stop somewhere for lunch."

"There's Paddy's Café just up the street."

"When we get there, we have a lot to talk about."

Flanna nodded and started off.

AS THEY WALKED down the street, Flanna replayed everything that had happened in her head. She could hardly believe she was involved in another crime not of her doing. Could hardly believe that *this* time she faced the possibility of being convicted and sent to prison. Michael wouldn't let that happen. And neither would she. Together, they would find the truth.

Convincing herself of that, Flanna felt as if she could breathe for the first time since they'd found Sean Hogan dead practically on her doorstep. Her relief was short-lived, however, for she spotted Barry Rafferty coming toward her, with Bridget's houseman, Hugh Nolan, following behind, juggling several packages.

"Don't stop," Michael murmured.

She nodded even as her pulse rushed through her, her automatic responses gearing up for a confrontation that she really would rather avoid.

But no one was able to avoid Barry Rafferty when he was on a tear.

He stepped directly in front of her and spat out, "What are you doing walking the streets like an innocent woman? Did you escape?"

Michael answered. "Murphy let us go because we're not guilty of anything."

"I don't believe it! What incompetence!"

Hugh put a hand on Barry's shoulder. "Mr. Barry, your blood pressure. Perhaps we should go on to—"

"Murphy should lock you up and throw away the key!"

Tired of the accusations, Flanna finally lost her temper. "I'm neither a thief nor a murderer, but perhaps the *garda* ought to be looking at you more closely, Barry Rafferty. You're full of steam. Bluff is what I call it. And why? What are you trying to cover up? If anyone had anything to gain from your mother's death, it would be you and your brother!"

"How dare you!"

"Mr. Barry…"

Hugh was trying to pull him away now, but Barry dug in

his heels, shrugged off the houseman's hand and looked ready to explode.

Before he could start in on her, Flanna said, "If it's the last thing I do, I will find the stolen jewelry and I will have the name of the real murderer...no matter how important he thinks he is. I'm a McKenna, remember. And whether or not you believe in my psychic gift, I *will* use it to bring all those involved to justice!"

Barry stormed off, leaving Hugh behind. The houseman appeared apologetic. "Sorry, Miss Flanna. I know this whole situation has been a trial for you."

"You're very kind, Hugh. Hopefully things will be resolved soon."

"Is there a break in the case?" he asked.

"Nothing official. But Michael and I have a lead." Michael's hand on her arm stopped her from continuing. "You'd better catch up to your new employer."

"Good luck to you, then." Hugh looked from her to Michael, nodded and moved off.

Now that the confrontation was over, Flanna felt her adrenaline quickly drain away.

"Do you think that was wise, antagonizing Rafferty?" Michael asked.

"He's a bully. I simply couldn't stand it any longer."

"The houseman seemed mighty interested in what's going on."

"And why wouldn't he be? Hugh was loyal to Bridget."

"I'm sure you're right. C'mon." His arm around her back, Michael gently swept her forward. "Let's get something to eat. You'll feel better."

Paddy's Café was a cheery, charming place with small tables, a counter with stools and a big glass case with take-away. It was also a busy place, but they lucked out in that they arrived after breakfast hours and just at the start of lunch. Only a few tables were currently occupied. Sitting toward the back, they placed their orders.

"I think I'm in a bit of shock," Flanna said. "I can hardly take it all in."

"We're making someone nervous."

"Nervous?"

"We're getting too close."

"Close? But we don't know anything."

"Maybe we do. Maybe the real killer knows we were trying to get information out of Travelers. And that person hired one to do his dirty work."

"There's definitely a mastermind behind this. This morning when I touched the ring, I saw someone hand it to Hogan."

"Who?"

"I don't know. I only saw Hogan and the hand…as if I was looking from the prospective of that person. The hand was covered with a glove with a small insignia on the wrist. I saw that glove before, Michael—on the hand holding the candle-stick that struck Bridget in the head."

Michael's expression shifted subtly. Flanna thought maybe he was starting to believe her.

"This insignia on the glove," he said. "What did it look like?"

"I couldn't quite make it out the first time, but this time I did. It looked like a little green shield with a red triangular flag."

"Do you recognize it?"

"I think I should…but I can't quite place it."

"Maybe it'll come back to you."

"It's there in my memory somewhere, but it keeps eluding me."

"Having memory problems?"

Flanna looked up to see Lisa Madden standing a yard away from their table.

"You know what they say," Flanna joked to cover, "the memory is the first thing to go."

"You're a little young for that."

"Are you meeting someone for lunch?" Flanna asked.

"Actually, I came in for some take-away. But if I could join you for a moment…"

Michael stood and pulled out a chair. "Please."

Lisa smiled at him as a woman smiles at a man she's attracted to. Flanna caught that. And to her surprise she didn't like it.

"I thought an apology was in order to you both," Lisa said.

Flanna asked, "For what?"

"I heard what happened to you this morning. I'm so relieved you weren't arrested."

"News travels fast around here," Michael said.

"It is a small town. At any rate, I'm sorry I told you about Sean Hogan."

"I don't understand," Flanna said.

"If Mr. Eagan hadn't gone after him for information, none of this would have happened."

"You don't know that," Michael said. "We came to you for help. You only told us about Hogan because you thought he had something to do with your good friend's murder. We can't hold you responsible."

"Well, thank you. At least there is some justice. A twisted criminal is off the streets, and Bridget can rest easier in her grave now."

"He didn't kill her," Flanna said, then felt Michael nudge her foot under the table. Again she realized he didn't want her to say more.

"Did Murphy tell you that?"

"No. It's just a feeling." Flanna shrugged, as if to diminish her original statement.

Lisa shuddered. "If you're correct, none of us is safe with a murderer on our streets. But Murphy is satisfied his case is solved."

"I'm not sure about that," Michael said.

"Really, now…" Lisa glanced over her shoulder and stood. "My order is ready. Again, I apologize. I'm just happy you're both all right."

Watching Lisa walk away, Flanna asked, "Did that seem odd to you? Her apologizing, I mean."

"I got the feeling she was on a reconnaissance mission. She wanted the latest on the official investigation and the apology was her way in."

"Cynical…but perhaps accurate."

The waitress brought them their food. Flanna dug in, relieved to get something in her stomach. Her mouth was stuffed when she realized Michael was watching her.

"You do have a healthy appetite."

She swallowed. "Is that a problem?"

"That was a compliment. Eat."

Flanna did. And she thought more about Lisa's apology. The tip on Sean Hogan had taken an unexpected turn, but she wasn't sorry for it. The vision she'd had on touching the ring could lead to something.

All she had to do was place that insignia….

"Our plan hasn't changed, has it?" she asked.

"As soon as we leave here, we'll see about renting a trailer for a few days."

"Good."

Flanna was anxious to get started.

The person behind the thefts and murders had obviously tried to set them up.

The next step in stopping them might be more drastic.

Chapter Nine

"We've lost nearly the whole day," Flanna complained as they set out in their truck and trailer. "Having to drive to Shannon to get it set us back."

On the way, they'd stopped at a thrift store to pick up some bargain-basement clothing more appropriate to poor Travelers. Her new yellow sundress was a little garish and clashed with her hair, which she'd put up with a clip, but it wouldn't raise suspicions. They'd also stopped for food staples. Flanna knew Travelers weren't welcome in a lot of places. Besides, if they found a camp for the night, there would be people to talk to, and maybe over a cook fire.

Assuming the Travelers didn't see through them.

"Think of it this way," Michael said. "We just bypassed the sites we already checked out. We can drive in any direction from here. We really only lost a few hours. With the trailer, we can sleep on the road and be ready to go on in the morning."

The trailer—she really didn't want to think too deeply on it. The space was tiny with a bench for two at an eating table, a small cooking area, a toilet—in which there was no curtain separating the shower from the rest of the tiny facility—and one double bed. They were pretending to be a married couple, but it was to be in name only. That was fine for daytime when they were driving or trying to get information from the real Travelers. It was nights that worried her. Circumstances would force them too close for her comfort.

Then there were the rings they now wore—thin gold bands they'd purchased at a pawnshop. It hurt her heart to know that people were so poor they had to sell their wedding rings to put food on the table. At least that's what she imagined they'd been about.

Looking at the band on her left ring finger, Flanna was reminded of the solemn vows normally attached to wearing one. Her dreams of love shattered, she'd mourned the idea of never wearing a wedding band before she'd put it out of mind altogether. Erin had so thoroughly destroyed her belief in real love that she'd put her mind to where it belonged—on her career.

Yet when Michael had slipped the ring on her finger, she'd imagined—just for a moment—that anything was possible. That is, until she remembered they were simply posing as man and wife. Attracted to each other they might be, but they were partners in an investigation, not in life.

She only hoped they weren't on a fool's errand. Too many things could go wrong.

"Do you think Murphy is going to go ballistic when he finds out we've left Killarra?" she asked.

"Afraid he's going to send the cavalry after us?"

"He might. I have this weird feeling…."

"If you want to change your mind, you need to do it now."

She didn't say she felt as if danger sat on their shoulders. Like the killer knew what they were up to. Michael would merely put it to her overactive imagination. And perhaps that was correct. Perhaps her nerves were so taut because she was dreading the close quarters she would share with him.

"I agreed to the plan," she said. Besides which, going

undercover was the only way they were going to get a lead on the thief and eventually on the murderer. "I'm not going to back out now."

Still, she couldn't shake the impending sense of doom. How could she when murder had been so close to home? Finding Sean Hogan dead that morning had certainly made a mess of her. Maybe her imagination was torturing her, but there was reason for it. Needing a distraction, she chose to amuse herself. And, hopefully, Michael.

"Do you see that rath there," she said, pointing to a farmer's field.

"Rath? You mean that mound?"

"Also known as a fairy fort. They're all over the country. Ancient Celts lived in raths surrounded by Druids' magic. Many Irish believe misfortune will fall upon them if they disturb the raths, so they leave them be. Farmers cultivate the land right around them."

"The Irish are very superstitious people."

"Does that include you?"

"I'm an American. But I remember my grandmother, who was born in Galway, held the superstitions. She was always talking about fairies. I figured it was a way of staying close to the land she left."

"When the Celts invaded, the occupants—the Tuatha Dé Danaan—were driven into hiding. They went underground, into the raths. Hidden, they were the speculation of the invaders, who made them smaller and smaller in their minds until they turned them into the fairy people. Of course the legends changed over the centuries. It's said fairies can change the seasons, weather, nature in general."

"My grandmother used to say fairies could enchant humans and hold them hostage in the fairy realm."

Flanna laughed. "Now that's the romantic in your grand-mother speaking. Not all fairies are enchanting with pretty, diaphanous wings. The pooka, for example, often appears as a dark horse with sulphurous yellow eyes and a long wild mane. It roams the countryside at night, damaging farms and scattering livestock."

Sheep dotted the landscape to her right as far as the eye could see. No pookas here. The land was so idyllic it almost lulled Flanna into thinking she was safe. Now that was an illusion if she ever had one. Her harboring the Celtic ring—she'd hidden it in a small bag attached to the inside waistline of her dress at the moment—guaranteed she wasn't safe until the killer was caught. Neither of them was. Perhaps she should have turned the ring over to Murphy. If she had done so, however, she would've had to live with the consequences if anyone else died because of it.

"So what's your plan to get information?" Michael asked. "I assume you have one."

"I'll spin a tale about a brother I'm trying to find. Liam Cary would be his name, though I will regretfully admit he goes under others. We've been estranged for the past year and now I want to reconnect with him."

"Estranged why?"

"Because of *you*. Liam didn't approve of you, Michael, didn't want me to have anything to do with you. And so we went out on our own. If it comes to it and anyone hears you speak, I'll use the fact that you're American. Not that Travelers are known to marry outside their own. But it does happen."

"So what's different? Why would you want to reconnect with him? Why would he take you back into the fold?"

Flanna felt heat creep up her neck. "Because I just learned I'm pregnant. A settled marriage partner is never accepted as a Traveler, but the children from that marriage would be. My brother can't keep my child from the clan."

"Will they buy it?"

"Travelers are all about family and keeping connections."

Not unlike the McKennas.

Where the idea for the baby had come from, Flanna wasn't sure, but once the plan occurred to her, she couldn't stop thinking about it. For years she'd avoided considering what she would lose if she remained alone all her life.

Strangely enough, the baby excuse made her long for something she didn't even know she wanted.

THEY'D BEEN ON the road for more than an hour, long enough for Flanna to enchant Michael with her fairy stories, when he spotted an RV pulled to the side of the road. A young woman who looked to be in her early twenties was sitting in a fold-out chair watching her three small children at play.

Before he could speak up, Flanna said, "Pull up in front of them. Then wait in the lorry."

"I'm not going to let you do this alone."

"Travelers aren't any more dangerous than settled people, Michael. I'll be fine and won't have to explain you."

Michael didn't like it, but he did as she wanted. He watched her walk back to the woman via the truck's side-view mirrors, though, and kept the window rolled down so he could hear.

"Good day to you," he heard Flanna say. "I'm wondering if you could help me. I'm trying to find my brother Liam Cary."

The woman's soft response was lost to Michael, but she didn't turn Flanna away.

He thought about the story Flanna had invented and imagined her with a baby in her arms. The thought put a smile to his lips. Everything about her made him smile. He'd never met a woman like Flanna McKenna, couldn't imagine ever meeting one like her again. She was unique. Her own person.

One he could see in his life…

"She hasn't seen him." Having opened the door without his realizing it, Flanna climbed into the truck. "But she said to keep going and when we get to the next crossroad, we should turn west and we'll find more of our people. Travelers, I mean."

"So she bought it all?"

"She believed my lies," Flanna said.

Not that she sounded happy. He suspected Flanna didn't like lying and that she was doing so only because the purpose was greater than her own feelings on the matter.

He respected her for it, and he wanted to put the smile back on her face.

"So, have you ever run in to a leprechaun?"

"Do I live like I've claimed a pot of gold?" she asked, sounding surprised at his whimsy. "They're guardians of ancient treasure left by the Danes as they swept through Ireland. Leprechauns tend to avoid foolish, greedy humans, and yet, if caught by a mortal, a leprechaun will promise great wealth if the human will set him free. Don't take your eyes off him, though, or he'll vanish like that." She snapped her fingers.

While Michael thought it all harmless nonsense, he was nevertheless enchanted by the teller. Flanna McKenna was like some beautiful creature from a past life—a colorful, yellow-garbed, reddish-haired fairy herself.

Every moment he spent with Flanna, Michael fell a little harder for her. He tried to resist her, but no matter his determination, she proved to be a distraction. He was finding it more and more difficult to keep his mind on the case.

He couldn't keep doing this.

He had to pay attention to every detail around them.

His biggest fear was missing something that would put them both in more danger.

It took the McKenna woman and her partner forever to get to the crossroad. For a while it seemed as if they would park for the night where they'd stopped.

The lorry and trailer turned left. West. A moment later, the watcher pulled from a stand of trees and followed.

The situation was getting serious. The plan to get rid of two problems at once hadn't played out the way it was supposed to. Right now, the two snoops should be locked up.

Instead, they were on the road, driving west to look for a thief and a murderer....

When all they had to do was look behind them.

Chapter Ten

As night fell, Flanna started giving up hope that her plan would work. Though she'd consulted the ring several times, it had given up no secrets.

In the midst of a rainstorm, they'd caught another lone RV parked on the side of the road. It had taken awhile for the rain to soften so that the occupants ventured outside. Next they came upon a trailer twice the size of theirs, carrying a large family.

Both times, she'd stuck to the women.

Both times, she'd struck out.

Neither had admitted to seeing anyone in the clan that wore the stallion tattoo.

Whether they were being truthful, she couldn't tell. The last woman had looked away furtively when she'd denied any knowledge of Flanna's supposed brother.

Her reaction meant the woman doubted her. Flanna was going to have to change her story a bit to suit the situation.

"Looks like the leprechauns were smiling on you, after all, Flanna. We hit the jackpot."

Michael indicated an open farmer's field where three trailers were camped together.

"Good. Probably these people are traveling together, part of the same clan, if not of the same immediate family. If no one objects to our stopping here, we'll have a place to camp for the night."

She wasn't so sure about getting information out of anyone. Three strikeouts—as Michael called them—had been disappointing to say the least.

"Let's find out."

As usual, he let her do the talking, and the leader of the clan agreed that they were welcome to share their camp. Asking questions could wait until later, until she'd established some trust. Going about their business—setting up their camp, making and eating dinner—would help convince the Travelers that they weren't anyone to cause worry.

Flanna started frying a simple dinner of potatoes, root vegetables and sausages, while Michael put up the awning on one side of the trailer via a nylon line, after which he then brought out their two fold-away chairs and small table.

"Smells good," he said, coming inside. "I could eat a snake."

"You know about the snakes in Ireland, don't you?" she asked. "There aren't any because St. Patrick drove them off into the sea. Well, all but one stubborn snake who refused to go."

"What did St. Patrick do?"

"Ah, he built a box and suggested the snake go inside, make himself a cozy home since he didn't want to leave," Flanna said. "The snake insisted it was too small and they began blathering, of course. Finally to prove he was right, the snake slithered into the box to show how tight the fit was. St. Patrick of course slammed down the lid and threw the box into the sea after the other snakes."

Michael laughed. "You have a story about everything. Is that a family trait?"

The workspace was so small that he was standing too close. Heat came at Flanna from dual directions—from the burner in front of her and from Michael behind her. Her pulse picked up and she had trouble taking a deep breath as she stirred the food in the iron skillet.

"I'm Irish, you know. We all have a bit of the blarney in us. We all like a good story."

"As far as I'm concerned, you can keep telling them. Until now, I never met a woman who made me smile so much."

Her heart suddenly demanded to be heard. It beat so hard it bumped up against her ribs. No man had ever said that to her before. They talked about her pretty face, fine figure, bright Irish eyes. Not about her smile.

"If you could get the dinner plates?"

"I'm on it."

He reached over her head to the shelf where the plates were fixed in place by a wedge of wood. That brought him even closer. His heat pressed up against her, making her melt inside.

Michael must have felt it, too. For a moment, as his body pressed against hers, he froze. All but for the area of his groin. A sudden growing pressure against her rear unnerved Flanna and she dropped the spatula.

"Lord, I'm clumsy," she mumbled, horrified that her body had responded instantly to his. Horrified that he might realize as much.

Michael pulled away immediately and set the plates on the small table. "I'm going to wait outside. Not enough room for two people in here."

Flanna couldn't agree more. Not unless those two people were naked and moving as one. The thought set an explosion of X-rated suggestions through her mind as she doled out the food and gathered the flatware.

She could hardly look at Michael as she called him to the

trailer doorway and handed him the plates. "Set these on the table and I'll get the tea."

Iced tea would help cool them right down, she thought, but she hadn't looked in the tiny freezer earlier to know the ice cube trays were empty. Cooled tea would have to do. She poured out two glasses and brought them outside.

Michael sat at the table waiting for her, but his gaze was on the other Travelers. She saw that they had gathered in a large group to share their evening meal. There was a real sense of community among the travelling people. Of family.

They ate in silence for a few moments. Then, in an effort to shake off the awkwardness she'd felt in the trailer, Flanna said, "You know quite a bit about me, Michael. It's time I learned something about you."

He swallowed a mouthful of food. "What's to tell? My business is poking my nose into other people's lives."

"No, not your work. You." Suddenly she wanted to know everything about him. "Your family."

"There's only Mom and me now—"

"Your father died?"

"Just before my eighteenth birthday."

"I'm so sorry. I can't imagine losing someone I love…and so young. But it's just you and your mother? You're the only child?"

His visage darkened. "I had a brother, but he died, too."

"How awful for you. What happened, if I may ask?"

"I don't like to talk about it. Sorry."

His tone held a note of finality that kept her from digging deeper. She concentrated on her food for a moment. Then something came to her—the way he often took out the pocket watch, the way he touched it as if it meant something to him when he didn't realize she was looking.

She couldn't stop herself from asking, "That pocket watch—was that your father's?"

"It was."

"How nice that you have something to remember him by."

"It keeps me on the straight and narrow."

An odd power to give an inanimate object, Flanna decided, but asking Michael to explain might upset him and she didn't mean to do that. He would undoubtedly explain when he was ready.

They finished eating in silence. By the time they were done, the numbers roaming the camp had diminished. The smaller children had been put down for the night. The women sat together outside of one trailer, the men outside another. The older children remained together and as far away from the adults as they could possibly manage.

"If you'll take care of the cleanup," Flanna said, "I'll go talk to the women."

"Good luck."

Thinking she would need it as well as an embellished story, Flanna set out to see if she could get any useful information.

The women welcomed her, yet were a bit reserved. One of them spoke using the Cant, commenting on the fact that Michael was doing the dinner cleanup. Thankfully, Flanna understood all but a few words. She, of course, told her lies in English.

"Yes, I have a thoughtful husband, made more so by the baby that's coming."

When she touched her belly as reverently as if she really were pregnant, Flanna felt an immediate pang of guilt. And longing. The second scared her more than the first.

Brought in by her lie, the women immediately softened and smiled at her, offering congratulations.

"Sit, sit," one said, indicating an empty chair. "I'm Mary and these are Rianne and Theresa."

"Flanna."

"So why are you out alone in your condition? Where is your family?"

"My parents are gone," she said, hating saying so when her da had already had a heart attack. She swallowed her reluctance and said, "There's only my brother. I've been looking for him to tell him the good news."

"You don't keep in touch?" Rianne asked.

"Liam doesn't approve of my Michael." Choosing not to explain that he wasn't Pavee like them unless they directly asked, Flanna looked from one woman to the other. "But now, with the baby coming…"

Mary clucked. "Surely he'll relent."

"If I can find him. Liam has a way of getting into trouble. He's—he's in trouble now." She shifted to a worried expression. "Another reason I have to find him."

"What kind of trouble?"

"He has a great deal of money that isn't his." Flanna figured that was probably true. He'd no doubt been paid well for his thieving work. "His name is Liam Cary, but sometimes he goes by other names." She touched her upper arm. "He wears the tattoo of the horsemen."

"What does he look like?" Mary asked.

"Liam has dark hair and he's not as fair-skinned as me." She knew that much from the vision. "Unless he's decided to become a redhead or some such nonsense in the way of disappearing." She gave the other women a brave smile.

"I saw a lad who fit that description yesterday—the dark hair, I mean—in a food mart," Theresa said. "And I noticed the tattoo right off. He picked out some very expensive beef cuts, and the butcher told him he couldn't afford it. The lad took out a roll of money this thick...." She held her forefinger and thumb open about three inches. "No apology from the butcher, of course."

Flanna feigned an even more pained expression and shook her head. Then she said, "That does sound like it could be Liam. Where were you when you saw him? Did you get any idea of where he was headed?"

"That was in Ballyloy. His name wasn't Liam, though. The girl he was with called him Joey and told him to hurry or they would never get to Dublin."

"And here we've been heading west, in the wrong direction altogether. No doubt my brother is already in Dublin."

And how they would find him in a big city was another question.

Theresa shook her head. "He couldn't be in Dublin. He won't be for weeks. He doesn't have a trailer or RV. He's driving one of the old horse-drawn caravans." Her expression changed slightly, and her eyes narrowed. "I'm surprised you didn't know that."

"Well, he didn't have a caravan when Michael and I married," Flanna said, trying to allay the woman's suspicion. "And I haven't seen my brother for nearly a year. But Liam always said if he got some money he was going to buy one. It looks like that's exactly what he did."

Knowing she'd better leave it alone, Flanna started asking questions about the women's families. How many children did they have? How old? Did they all get along? She played the anxious, soon-to-be mother, asking advice to discourage any suspicions.

Soon it was too late for talking. The men broke up and called their women to their trailers.

And Flanna went to hers.

As she stepped inside, Michael came out of the bathroom, shirtless, his face dotted with shaving cream.

"I had to do something to distract myself or go nuts." He wiped his face clean with a towel as he moved closer. "How did it go?"

Flanna tore her gaze from the broad expanse of naked chest that was too close for comfort and met his eyes.

"I'm thinking we have a lead. One of the women saw a man with the stallion tattoo in Ballyloy yesterday. He's traveling with a woman in a horse caravan. They're in a hurry to get to Dublin."

"If they're in a hurry, they should've given up the caravan." Michael smiled and his face lit up. "Lucky for us they didn't. We should be able to catch up with him tomorrow."

"My thoughts exactly. Oh, and his woman called him Joey."

Suddenly his hands cupped her shoulders. "You should congratulate yourself for a job well done." He pulled her to him for a hug.

Flanna caught her breath as every inch of her that touched him overheated.

"Yes…well…I would feel better without the lies," she said. "After getting nowhere telling the truth, I realize they were necessary if we're to get justice for the murdered women."

A longing that she hadn't felt in years filled her. She wanted to close her eyes and let him hold her…kiss her again…touch her more intimately… She slid her hands along his sides, felt the well-developed muscles of a man who worked out. She wanted to touch all of him.

He let go of her as suddenly as he'd pulled her to him, as if he were uncomfortable with her discomfort.

"Keep that goal in mind and you'll get through this," he assured her. "No one would think less of you for it."

"It's just that I was betrayed by someone I cared for."
Why she felt the need to explain, she couldn't say. "He
wasn't at all what I thought he was. He used lies to get what
he wanted and then—"

"Left you?"

"No, I left him." She'd done more than left Erin. She had
blown the whistle on him, but he'd gotten away before the authorities could investigate. "He probably would have stayed
with me until he used me up. Mentally," she added. She
thought about telling Michael the whole story, but he considered her gift another fairy tale like the ones she'd told him on
the road. "You simply wouldn't believe me."

He didn't say anything for a moment, and she wondered
if he was going to pursue the unbelievable anyway. But when
he spoke, it was to reassure her.

"I'm sorry you had that experience, but this isn't the same
thing. You're not hurting anyone, Flanna. Just the opposite.
You're trying to stop a criminal. Probably two. You're trying
to prevent anyone else from being hurt."

"The end justifying the means."

Michael didn't say anything, simply stood there, too sym-
pathetic, too close.

He was holding himself back. She could feel it. And she
needed to do the same. Getting personally involved would
be a mistake. For them both. There simply was no future in
it for them.

She said, "I should get ready for bed if you're through with
the facilities."

"Go ahead. You do know there's only one bed." Before she
could figure out how to respond, he said, "I checked out the
bench here to see if I could sleep on it somehow." He indi-

cated the padded seating at the small table. "Half of my legs would hang over."

"Mine wouldn't. I can sleep there."

"I wouldn't hear of it. You get the bed."

"What about you, then?"

"I'll take a sleeping bag outside."

"It will likely rain." Pretty much a sure thing in this part of the country.

"I'll sleep under the canopy, and if rains hard, I'll come inside. Not that I'm worried over the possibility. I'll wake you at dawn and we'll get an early start after this Joey character. Hopefully this charade will be over by dusk and you won't have to tell any more lies."

Flanna nodded. She let him get a T-shirt and the sleeping bag and leave the trailer before she used the facilities and changed into the shorts and T-shirt she'd brought for sleep.

Climbing into the bed, it suddenly seemed too big and lonely for her. A part of her wished that Michael had suggested sharing it. The other part knew lying with him could quickly become incendiary...and give her reason for regret later. She didn't sleep around. When the only man she'd ever given herself to had betrayed her, she'd put aside her physical needs. And that's where they should stay.

Sharing herself should mean something, should be a commitment of sorts. How could she commit herself to a man who wouldn't be around a month from now?

Besides which, Michael might like and be attracted to her, but he didn't respect her gift, which meant he didn't respect her—not any more than Erin had. The men were very different and their takes on her gift of touch were direct opposites, but neither was acceptable.

It was no wonder she'd closed her heart from accepting

Gran's legacy. Only when a man held all of her in esteem
would she be able to rethink her position.

THE AMERICAN was standing guard for the McKenna
woman again.

What else could be surmised by his sleeping outside the
trailer?

Bad enough that they'd camped for the night with a group
of Travelers. Witnesses. A reason to keep counsel, to delay
taking action.

The longer the wait, the less likely they would catch up to their
quarry. If they kept going west, that would be never. They would
spin their wheels and Begley would disappear into the mists.

Then, with Beltane and the potential of obtaining a
powerful witch's magic only a few days away, all that needed
to be done was to get the ring to complete the suite.

Even if the McKenna woman had to die for it.

Chapter Eleven

MacNeil's Mart was just opening when they arrived in Ballyloy the next morning. Michael waited in the car while Flanna went inside to see what she could learn. The butcher counter was still closed and the only person in the store was the clerk at the register.

She did a little shopping then brought her basket to the counter. The clerk barely looked at her as he rang up the items and bagged them.

"I'm hoping you can help me," Flanna said.

"What do you need?"

"I'm looking for my brother Joey."

"What's that to me?"

"I know he passed through Ballyloy yesterday. Since this is the only food mart in town, I assumed he stopped here to stock up."

"I wouldn't be knowing that. I didn't work the register yesterday."

"Who did?"

"My sister Connie."

"Is it possible for me to speak to her?"

The man gave her a put-upon look, then shouted, "Connie, get out here!"

A door opened. "What're you blathering about, Donal?"

"A customer wants to speak to ya."

By the time Flanna paid for her goods, Connie had come out from the back.

Giving Flanna a thorough once-over and obviously assuming she was a Traveler, the woman kept her distance. "What do you want?" she asked coolly.

Even though she was pretending to be something she was not, the attitude stung Flanna a bit.

"I'm trying to catch up with my brother Joey. I know he came through Ballyloy yesterday and he would have stopped to restock his groceries."

"A lot of people came through here yesterday."

"He has dark hair and a tattoo with a stallion's head on his arm."

The clerk was silent for a moment, then said, "Ah, that one. He was here midmorning, I think. Is that it, then?" She turned to go.

"I know he's on his way to Dublin, but did he say anything about which route he was taking out of town?"

Connie looked back, her gaze narrowed on Flanna. "Now why do you think I would be interested in the wanderings of one of your people?"

Flanna feigned hurt. "I—I just thought he might have mentioned it." And made up yet another lie. "Our mam is sick and he doesn't know it. I have to catch up to him, bring him to her before it's too late. Please…"

The other woman's hard features softened a bit, and with an expulsion of breath, she relented. "The lad said something about needing to get to O'Briensbridge. I pointed him in the right direction, but I don't think he intends to take a national road."

He undoubtedly wouldn't, not with a horse-drawn caravan.

Instead, he would take back roads that cut across the country in as straight a line as he could. At least they had a direction, which cut down their search by more than half. O'Briensbridge was a village on the east bank of the River Shannon and, as its name implied, had a bridge over the river into Co. Limerick. Thanking the woman profusely, she took her bag of groceries and left the store.

Michael stood outside the lorry, stretching his legs. When he saw her, he straightened. "Any luck?"

As she told him what she'd learned, Flanna caught sight of a black Mercedes parked on the other side of the street. Even as instinct made her take a better look, the vehicle pulled away from the curb. Flanna frowned.

Where had she seen that car before?

She didn't have time to think about it. They set off immediately, Michael driving as usual, Flanna navigating using a local map. Several regional roads connected small towns along the way. The roads tended to be quite narrow and winding in places, but were better for a horse-drawn caravan than the national roads. There were many more boreens—even smaller, unclassified roads, paved cow-paths with hedgerows or limestone fences on either side. He could be on any one of these, as well.

Which one was the question.

They drove with the windows open, and as they went down a narrow road, thick hedgerows surrounded them on both sides, while mature-growth trees arched over them so driving on it was like shooting through a tunnel. From somewhere nearby, the mournful sound of Uilleann pipes drifted to them.

"Now if you have any whimsy in you, Michael Eagan, imagine the pipes are being played by a changeling."

"Is that another type of fairy?"

"Aye. One born stunted or deformed. Fairies love beauty above all, and since the wee creature is born without it, it often finds the beauty in music—in playing the Irish pipes or the fiddle."

The stories were rolling off her tongue with less fluidity this morning. Flanna felt a bit strung out and she was having difficulty splitting her focus. They were close to the thief, she sensed, and yet were having no luck in running him down. They spent hours going in circles, up one road, down the other, passing farm equipment and cars and lorries and even a Traveler vehicle or two.

Just not the one they were trying to find.

"I need a break," Michael finally admitted, pulling over to the side of the road. "And food."

The spot was so pretty, they decided to picnic. Taking the prepared meal she'd bought at the mart, Flanna led the way to the bank of a meandering stream. Around them, lush green hills rolled and dipped into thickly forested areas.

They ate at the edge of the stream. Flanna couldn't resist taking off her shoes and dipping her toes in the cold water like she had as a child. Well, as a child, she would have dipped her whole self, clothes and all.

"'Tis cold, but it feels grand," she said, wiggling her feet in water as she munched on her sandwich.

"Be careful some fish doesn't come along and nibble on your toes."

"What? Is that a bit o' whimsy coming from you, Michael Eagan?"

He smiled. "Maybe it's catching."

It was a perfect afternoon. Too bad they couldn't stay the day. Too bad thievery and murder had to drift in and out of her mind.

All too soon, they started off on their quest once more.

The thief had to be in the area somewhere. Flanna calculated the caravan couldn't be more than twenty miles from Ballyloy, probably less, considering how much weight the horse was pulling. But where? No matter how many back roads they took, and how many people—both settled and other Travelers—they asked, they still came up short, almost as if the thief knew they were looking for him and was hiding.

All the while, Flanna found her attention wandering back to the sharing, to the attraction building between her and Michael. For a few moments, he'd seemed like a different person—not a man putting on the charm to impress her mother or someone he wanted information from, but a truly charming man. For a few moments, he'd made her forget their purpose. Her past.

This was a man she wanted to get to know better.

Finally, at sunset, no closer to finding their quarry than they had been at dawn, they agreed to give up for the day.

They were looking for a nice place to camp for the night when Michael said, "Flanna, I know you're going to hate this, but we may have to sit at O'Briensbridge and just wait for this Joey character to show up."

"But that'll take him another day. Maybe two." Flanna's sense of urgency had revved up since that morning. "I have a bad feeling about this, Michael. I don't think we can wait that long."

"I didn't say we'd give up our search. I just meant we could be more realistic."

"All right, perhaps we need to head for O'Briensbridge in the morning."

Michael slowed the vehicle and pointed to a crumbling structure high on a hill. "Hey, what's that?"

At the top of the hill sat the ruins of a medieval castle that hadn't been all done up for tourists. A small boardwalk halfway up held a single bench facing the ruins, as well as a sign on a two-board fence that explained the castle's origins. Flanna had seen other sites like it, but this was possibly the most striking of them all.

"'Tis a castle ruin, of course."

"Of course."

Michael pulled the trailer alongside the foot of the hill, stopping in an open area with a perfect view of the enclosure fortified by a centuries-old wall. Two towers sat within the ruins, one with a gabled roof. The other, closer to the slope, was cut with defensive features—narrow slit windows, gun loops and murder holes. Farther back, yet another building was partially visible.

The sun sat low in the sky, sending streaks of red and orange and pink along the horizon. The ruins looked to be forming from some magical spell. The loveliness of the site took away Flanna's breath. It was a perfect romantic setting.

Then reality set in as she remembered.

In name only...

She and Michael weren't really a couple and there was nothing romantic about their chasing a thief through the Irish countryside.

She wished it was more.

"There's a fire ring over there." As they left the lorry, Michael pointed to a spot partially up the hill. "We could have a regular barbecue...um, cookout. What do you think?"

"I think it sounds grand."

Flanna put on a good face, and together they set up for the night, raising the canopy, setting out the chairs and small table, all the while talking about everyday things.

Whoever had last used the fire ring had left a bunch of stacked wood, and while Flanna fetched the food and utensils,

Michael set up the fire. Then, while she cooked, he got a blanket for them to sit on and a couple of pints of local brew from the refrigerator.

Michael spread out the blanket on a level area and Flanna lit a couple of candles in glass holders. Night fell quickly, but the moon was full, sending a silver-blue glow across the land and the ruins, so they could see all clearly as they ate.

What a spectacular view!

They were halfway through their meal and Flanna was considering how grand it was that they were alone, when the thought suddenly made her uneasy. Perhaps they should have joined a group of Travelers for the night…not that she wanted to trade this experience for something safe. Yet every time she heard something skitter below, she couldn't help but look around. She saw nothing amiss. Nerves, she thought. No one knew where they were, or what they were about.

Michael suddenly jerked her from the dark place only to send her to another. "That guy who used you up…how?" he asked. "What did he do to betray you?"

Normally, she chose not to think about Erin Cassidy, certainly didn't care to speak of him. This was different. She didn't know why she wanted to tell Michael about the most painful thing that had ever happened to her, especially in the face of his disbelief, but she did.

"My home is in Dublin. That's where I met Erin. In a pub in Temple Bar a few blocks from my flat. He was a musician. Exciting, talented…and full of the blarney."

"Sounds like you were a good match."

"I thought we were, especially since Erin not only accepted my gift but claimed to want to know everything extraordinary that had ever happened to me. Soon after we started seeing each other, he was out of work and broke, so we took one of his old guitars to a pawnshop. He saw my interest in an antique brooch in the case and insisted I had to see it up close."

"You got one of your visions?" Michael guessed.

"Aye."

She noticed he didn't say "supposed visions." In fact, he appeared less speculative than usual. Flanna didn't believe that Michael suddenly believed in her gift of touch, but at least he seemed open to the story.

"Go on," he said, sliding a hand across the blanket to cover hers, as if he were trying to hand her the courage to continue.

"It became a game with us over the next weeks. We would go into pawnshops and secondhand places and Erin would encourage me to find the stories in the pieces. A jeweled mirror, a humidor, an Asian vase. I thought it was all harmless fun—and it was for the most part. But some things I touched had histories too dark for my liking and I stopped wanting to play." She sighed. "And when I refused to continue, Erin stopped wanting to see me."

Flanna closed her eyes for a moment and took a deep breath so she could get it all out.

The next thing she knew, Michael slid closer, wrapped a comforting arm around her and said, "You don't have to say anything. I didn't mean to cause you pain."

A yearning she couldn't put words to filled Flanna and she settled closer to Michael. The warmth and strength of his body were comforting and gave her courage.

"I want to finish. I've only told the story twice, and that was five years ago—once to the authorities, the other to my sister Keelin. Perhaps I've needed to talk about it, to figure out how I let this happen."

"If that's what you need to do."

Nodding, Flanna said, "I had the key to Erin's flat and so

I went there to wait for him, to ask him what had changed. The week before I'd left some things behind and I decided to fetch them, so I wouldn't have to stay to find them later if things were bad between us."

Flanna swallowed hard as the nightmare unfolded before her eyes once more. She could still see it, feel the cold in the pit of her stomach, the emptiness in her heart.

"When I opened the closet I found a music box, a Tiffany lamp, enameled opera glasses—all things…"

"Things you'd found together that had a lot of value?"

"Yes."

"He went back and bought them?"

"No. He stole them. He made me an unknowing accessory to his thievery, Michael, and when I stopped giving him what he wanted, he no longer needed me. Maybe that's why I'm so set on finding the thief who stole Bridget's jewelry." A shiver ran through her as she thought he could be somewhere close and they wouldn't even know it. "I was helpless in the face of Erin's betrayal. But maybe I can make up for it now. If we find the thief, maybe we can find the murderer. I can't explain why, but I feel this overwhelming sense of responsibility—"

Michael cupped her chin and turned her face to his so that he could look straight into her eyes. "You weren't at fault. Not for what happened to Bridget. Not for what Erin did to you."

"But I not only accepted Erin into my life, I wanted him more than anything. I didn't stop to think about why he was so fascinated with me…to realize that he had an ulterior motive…"

"The only thing you were guilty of was having an open heart and a trusting soul."

"I wish that was true."

"It is. I know it is," he murmured, brushing his lips over hers. When she didn't protest, he deepened the kiss.

In Name Only?

Emotions she'd been denying for too long flooded her, and Flanna threw herself into Michael's embrace as a starving woman would devour a banquet. She opened herself up to longing…to joy…to desire.

Michael pressed her backward into the blanket. Slowly he ran his hand from the side of her waist to the flat of her stomach to her breast. Sensations swamped her. Those, too, had been locked up tight lest she make another foolish mistake.

But Michael was no mistake, she told herself. He was honest and trustworthy, nothing at all like Erin. She'd been holding back out of fear, but she had reason to fear no longer. Not with Michael.

He might indeed be Gran's legacy come true.

They were a married couple in name only, but Flanna now wondered what that might be like in truth. What would life be like if Michael were, indeed, her husband?

When his hand slipped down between her thighs, she pulled up the skirts of her dress to give him access.

He touched her…stroked her…brought her to a damp frenzy…

She lifted her hips and helped him remove her panties, then found the zipper on his trousers and found and stroked him as intimately as he did her. Not willing to wait until he undressed, she pulled him over her, opened her legs and pushed against his tip until he sank inside her. Then Michael rolled to his back, taking her with him, so she sat astride him.

Connected yet still dressed, Flanna felt a giggle bubble up inside her.

"If it's a fairy story you're going to tell me, it had better be a sexy one," Michael warned.

"I'm thinking of an Aisling—an old poem called "The

Midnight Court"—that was so explicit it was banned. The teller is brought to a fairy court filled with unfulfilled females."

"So tell me."

"Why don't I show you instead?"

Flanna moved in short, slow strokes, her hands going to the V of her thighs. Through the dress, she touched herself, gasping at the sensations that flooded her. Then she moved with even more determination.

Before she knew what he was about, Michael slipped his hands under her skirts, slid them along her thighs until he found her juices and stroked the tender flesh until she was drenched.

Flanna threw back her head and opened herself to a man—truly, fully, emotionally, physically—for the first time in too many years.

The moment she gave up all control, she was well and truly caught. Her head began to spin as sensation flooded her and built and built until she gasped and froze. Her world lit and spun until she exploded from within. Michael cried out and grabbed her to him, wrapping his arms around her back as if he would hold her forever.

Chapter Twelve

Michael held Flanna in his arms, astounded at what had happened between them, not because he hadn't been attracted to her all along—and she the same—but because their love making had come out of her trusting him with her past.

Now why couldn't he trust her?

As if she could read his thoughts, she said, "Perhaps I told you too much before."

"It's all right," he said, wanting to protect her. "You didn't do anything wrong."

"Trusting Erin was—"

"A mistake," he finished for her.

"You have to believe me, Michael, that I would never knowingly connect myself to someone who'd committed criminal acts."

Michael went cold inside and he clung to her with an unfamiliar vehemence. He didn't want her to look at him with disdain or worse. If he trusted her—if he told her the truth about himself—that *would* be the end of them. She wouldn't be involved with someone who'd committed crimes.

Someone like him.

Flanna's hurt had gone so deep, he didn't think the circumstances, or the fact that he had changed, would make any difference to her. Perhaps if she had known before… But now it would seem like yet another betrayal to her. The truth would devastate her.

The last thing he wanted to happen.

This *was* the end of them. Had to be. He forced himself to see that. He would keep his own counsel and find another way— a hurtful way, because how could it be otherwise—to end what had just begun. No matter his own desires, he would put her first.

He couldn't live with any more guilt.

Steeling himself, he let go of Flanna and sat up. "Another brew?" He offered her a bottle of ale.

"No, thanks, I'm good." A happy grin lighting her face, she sprawled back on her elbows. "But if you have a thirst, then you must quench it."

She wiggled provocatively and he knew exactly what thirst she wanted quenched. His groin tightened. He wanted it, too. He could imagine taking her in every way possible and not tiring of her.

Would he be wrong if he let this go on until he had to return to Boston? Then he could simply get on a plane and leave Flanna behind.

His gut knotted. He couldn't do that. The longer they were together, the more hurt she would be.

"Those fairies had various ways to relieve their lustful natures," she teased, reaching out a foot and running her toes over his thigh.

And he would like to experience every one of them. Instead of taking her up on her blatant offer, he popped the top off the bottle of ale and took a swig.

"That's what I like about you the most, Flanna McKenna. Your very vivid imagination. Fairies and visions and a legacy that guides you."

Her smile faded and she sat upright. "Don't be besmirching Gran's legacy now. I have two siblings and five cousins who can attest to the truth of it."

Michael laughed. "But not you, right? Even you don't believe in that silliness."

"Silliness? I might not believe in the legacy, but it was Gran's dying wish for her nine grandchildren to find true love. You think her wishes are silly?"

"You know what I mean."

"No, I really don't." She got to her feet, found her panties and pulled them on, keeping her skirts draped so he couldn't see anything tantalizing. "I fear I've misjudged you." Then she found her shoes and slipped them on her feet.

"Oh, come on, lighten up."

She stood still, her expression crestfallen. "Why are you being so mean?"

"Not mean." He took another swig of ale—this one almost choked him. "Honest."

Flanna swallowed a low shriek and, to his surprise, turned and fled up the hill toward the castle ruins. The fence didn't stop her; she merely ducked through the opening between boards. Michael started to follow and then realized she might see that as him trying to make up with her.

No matter that he might want to, it would be better for her if he left it alone. If he let her cool off for a while.

Then, if he were smart, he would pretend that nothing had happened between them, that he hadn't fallen for her, and go back to the way things were.

They'd catch a thief, and then a murderer, and then he'd take himself back to Boston where he could nurse his ailing heart.

HER HEART BREAKING, the full moon lighting her way, Flanna ran up the uneven path to the castle ruins. Once she got there, then what? It wouldn't make her feel better. She only knew she had to get away from Michael for the moment.

She had to think…to consider why things had gone badly between them so quickly.

From the first, she'd known they were too different. He hadn't believed in her visions. He'd been humoring her, allowing her to tell him fairy stories. And now he'd shown contempt for the legacy left to her by a woman who was still dear to her heart a decade after her death.

When had she started believing in the McKenna Legacy?

To her chagrin, probably the moment she'd met Michael Eagan or very soon thereafter. She hadn't wanted to believe in the legacy, hadn't wanted to believe in love again, but apparently want and will were at war in her.

Her feelings for Michael frightened her. She'd let go for a brief moment, but the argument had brought her back to reality. He wasn't the man for her. They'd simply been thrown together by a tragic event. A series of crimes that Michael swore to solve. Perhaps that's why she was so attracted to Michael—because he was everything opposite of Erin. Perhaps she'd needed him—needed to be with him just this once—so that she could start over, find a man who suited her.

So why did this rift hurt so much?

She called herself every kind of fool for opening herself and her past to a stranger. How was she going to face Michael after this?

Gradually, as if coming out of a trance, Flanna awakened to her surroundings. She'd gone deep into the ruins and could see the place was a disaster, the reason it had been fenced off from the public. Well, the thinking public. She hadn't been thinking at all when she'd run from Michael. She'd been acting on pure instinct.

All around her, piles of rubble lay everywhere, smaller stones making the path uneven, and walking treacherous. That she had gotten this far without tripping and falling was sheer luck.

She turned to go back and carefully picked her way several yards before she heard the noise that made her stumble. The sound of a loose stone skipping on a nearby pathway was enough to unnerve her, to remind her of the potential danger involved in their search. Though her pulse picked up and she froze for a moment, she told herself Michael had come after her. Staying where she was, she waited for him to call out to her.

Seconds ticked by…and then a minute…and then another loose stone bounced against the walls, the echo going straight up her spine.

Thinking that Michael had decided to watch over her without letting her know, she finally called out to him. "Michael, where are you?" When he didn't immediately answer, she called louder, "Michael?"

No answer, but a footfall closer than the first.

Surely Michael would answer her…if it was Michael!

And surely someone with innocent intentions would call out to assure her, as well.

Flanna didn't need to be psychic to know she was in trouble, She turned and moved swiftly—silently, she hoped—in the opposite direction from the footfalls. She moved more by feel than by sight. While the moon was still full, she fled into the shadow of the higher tower and, hoping to disappear from view, tucked herself into a crevice.

Concentrating, listening, Flanna waited.

For a moment, she heard nothing…and then a nearby

crunch of gravel set her heart pounding so hard that she swore whoever was out there could hear its beat.

Her stalker passed by so close she could touch him, and yet she dared not chance a look. Waiting until the footsteps faded, she slipped out of the hiding place and retraced her path once more.

Which way to go? She didn't remember the path she'd taken. She'd been too upset to take notice. Now she had to rely on pure instinct. At the end of the tower, she turned left, but she didn't get far before realizing she was facing a dead end. The passageway was blocked by a pile of rubble.

That's when she heard the stalker somewhere behind her. Now the only way out was past him…or into the tower itself.

How safe would that be?

Choosing the unknown as the lesser of two evils, Flanna slipped through a doorway and moved swiftly toward the other side, hoping for another exit. This tower had no roof, and moonlight filtered in so that she could see an open-sided stone stairway, which fell off to a dark maw. A pit of some sort?

If there was another exit…where?

Hesitating long enough to look around so as not to miss anything, she glanced back as her stalker filled the doorway. He'd dressed in black with a dark, hooded mask that covered his face to conceal his identity. Was this the Joey they'd been tracking down? Had he somehow known they were following and therefore had lain in wait?

Having no other choice, Flanna started up the stairs, trying to keep her feet moving as fast as her heart was pounding.

When she got to the top, then what?

She'd barely gone up a dozen or so stairs when the man caught up to her and grabbed her from behind, swinging her around to face him.

Flanna screamed, "Michael! Help!" and fought the attacker for all she was worth.

Her bigger and stronger attacker captured one of her hands and twisted it high behind her back, making her smallest movement painful.

"The ring!" he demanded in a low, unrecognizable whisper. "Give it over!"

When she merely struggled against the pain, he wedged himself up against her, trapping her against the tower wall, and with his free hand, he began to body-search her, starting by plunging inside the top of her dress and mauling her breasts.

"No!" she screamed, slashing out at the hooded face with hooked fingers, hoping at least to remove the mask.

He let go of her and slashed out in return, smacking Flanna in the side of the head. Her world lit up from within and her knees caved. The next thing she knew she was on her back on the stairs, and he was hovering over her, his hands reaching for her. She couldn't let the thief get his hands on the ring. Too much was at stake if the jewelry suite was completed.

Gathering every ounce of strength she had left, she kicked out and jammed her foot as hard as she could into his knee. His curse was low, his purpose clear as he came at her again, his fist raised.

Then, suddenly, he jerked and stumbled back down a few steps, and Flanna realized she didn't have to fight the bastard alone. Michael pummeled the masked man.

Flanna got to her feet and tried to see what was happening as the men rolled into the shadows. Even with the moon doing its best to light the interior, there were so many dark crevices. The men were in full body contact, dancing around each other to get the lead. Though she couldn't see much, she heard the traded blows and the slap of leather on uneven stairs. The men grunted and groaned and whipped around in some kind of connected frenzy.

Thinking she had to do something to help Michael, Flanna felt along the stairs for a couple of good-sized stones. When the men whipped apart, she pitched them at the attacker with as much strength as she could muster. One stone struck him in the arm, the other in the head.

He howled and threw out an elbow, catching Michael in the chest and sending him reeling backward.

To Flanna's horror, Michael teetered at the edge of the open stairs, tried to catch his balance, then pitched backward with a surprised shout.

"Michael!"

Grabbing more stones, Flanna flung them at the attacker, driving him down the stairs with her following after him. The man turned his back on her, covered his head with his arms for protection and stumbled toward the exit.

Even as he pitched out of the tower, Flanna was circling the pit, trying not to panic.

"Michael, are you all right?" When she got no answer, terror welled in her, cutting off her breath. "Michael, say something, please!"

It was too dark to see much, other than his pale shirt. She was certain he was knocked out.

"C'mon, wake up! You've got to get out of there before he comes back!"

His response was a moan, but at least he was alive!

"You have to get up, Michael, grab onto anything, get a foothold somehow."

He didn't answer.

Flanna split her attention between the pit and the doorway, which remained empty. Below, Michael moaned again, but he didn't seem to be able to regain consciousness, let alone get to his feet. This was her fault. Again. If she hadn't run up here, she would never have left herself open to the attack, and Michael wouldn't have had to come after her. He wouldn't be trapped, maybe badly hurt.

"The bastard is gone, Michael, but I need you to wake up so we can get you out of there."

Though she didn't know how. As her eyes adjusted to the dark, she could see sheer drops on every side of the pit that ran about a dozen feet to the floor below.

"Michael, I don't want to leave you, but I've got to get help." Hopefully he could hear her and process what she was saying. "I have no choice. Even if you could get up and reach my hand, I'm not strong enough to lift you out of there."

Michael moaned again as if he were finally coming to. Had he understood anything she'd said?

"He could come back for you, Michael. I have to get help before he does."

"Could get you, too," he muttered. "Careful…don't want you hurt because of me…."

Flanna wanted to argue that all this was *her* fault, but that would simply waste time.

Heavy with guilt, she said, "I'm going. I'll be back as quickly as I can."

Before leaving the safety of the tower, she picked up several stones. Thankfully her brother Curran had taught her to throw a ball properly. Who would ever have thought that skill set would protect her life?

Moving fast through the ruins, she split her concentration between looking for new danger and coming up with a rescue plan. She didn't have a cell phone to call for professional help, and leaving the site to go in search of other people simply wasn't an option. She needed to find a rope so she could get down to Michael.

Rope…or nylon line like the one that raised the canopy. How long was it? It didn't matter. Whatever the length, it would have to do.

As she passed the fire pit, she stopped to dump both her stones and eating utensils—more effective protection—in a bag. She headed for the trailer.

Unthreading the nylon line from the canopy wasn't nearly as easy as she'd hoped. The knots confounded her and she was glad to have the utensils. One of the tines of the fork was the perfect fit to loosen the knots.

Within minutes, she was on her way back to the tower with the nylon line looped over her shoulder.

The closer she came to the tower, the more her muscles tightened and the more her chest squeezed the air out of her lungs. Michael had to be okay. He just had to. She had to get him out of that pit and to some place of safety.

Even though she was fairly certain the attacker had fled, she tuned in to every night noise, searched every shadow as she swiftly moved through the ruins.

At last she entered the tower. "Michael, are you still conscious?"

"I'm fine. I'm sure I'll be sore in the morning, but nothing is broken."

Kneeling over the pit, she was able to take a look at him for herself. He was on his feet now, his muscles bunched as if he wanted to hit something.

Or someone.

"I got the nylon line from the canopy," she told him. "I was thinking to secure it to one of the staircase supports and come down to help you."

"No, I'll come up. I told you I'm all right. Let's hope it's long enough."

No argument from her. Flanna was relieved Michael seemed to be himself again. After securing the line to the support, she tied a knife to the other end, both as ballast for the light line and as a weapon should Michael need it. She prayed the line or her knots wouldn't give under Michael's weight.

"Ready?" she asked.

"Let it down."

She began lowering it. "Can you see it?"

"I'm following your voice. If it reaches far enough, I'll find it."

Her greatest fear was that it wouldn't. Flanna held her breath until Michael called out again.

"I can't quite get my fingers on it. And there's nothing here for me to stand on. Do you have anything with you to make it longer?"

"No, but I'll find something. I'll be back as soon as I can."

Tucking a weapon into the waist of her dress, Flanna began the trek back to the trailer. Halfway there, she got an idea. Michael could reach the line if he had something to stand on. Stopping at the boardwalk, she found and pried free a loose plank. It wasn't even as high as her chin, but it was wide enough to support a man's foot.

Back to the tower.

This had to work. It *would* work.

She lowered the board down to him. "Try propping it against the wall. You can climb a few feet higher."

He set it at an angle against the wall as suggested, then adjusted it until it was secure. He climbed onto it and snaked his hand up toward the line.

"Got it!" he said. And when she picked it up at the end of

the pit, he ordered, "Stand back! Don't touch it. If something goes wrong, it'll rip you up."

"You can pull yourself up?"

"You think you're strong enough to haul my weight?"

A rhetorical question. She stepped back as Michael scrabbled against the wall and began to pull himself nearly straight up. Her heart was with him every inch of the way. And when she saw his head appear above the opening, she shook with relief.

Getting herself together, Flanna darted forward and grabbed Michael and tugged with all her might.

A moment later he clambered up onto the edge and then fell straight into her arms.

Chapter Thirteen

"He wasn't wearing gloves."

Flanna remembered the detail as she and Michael picked their way through the ruins on their way back to camp. Grasping the nylon line that she'd looped over her shoulder, she tried to keep her mind on the investigation and off that moment when they'd reconnected. Her emotions had been intense, had gone past mere relief that she had managed to rescue him.

"And that's significant how?" Michael asked, placing his hand at the small of her back to guide her.

Another shot of longing passed through her, but she steeled herself against giving in. "Just that we're still dealing with more than one person. That whoever attacked us isn't the killer."

"Because he wasn't wearing gloves."

"Exactly. Bridget's murderer was, as was the person who gave Sean Hogan the ring," Flanna said, remembering the vision and the insignia on the wrist that still eluded her. "But not the man who robbed the cottage."

"Joey, the Traveler we've been following, does seem the likely attacker."

"But he's not a killer, Michael. He was wanting the ring is all." She patted the bulge just below her waist where it still sat in its pouch. "Thankfully, he didn't get it."

"I could have died falling into that pit."

"You know he didn't try to kill you, though. Or me. Once you fell, that was it."

Though thankful that Michael was safe and basically unharmed, she still wanted to forget their earlier impulsiveness, to forget the emotions washing through her. The sight of their trailer, the canopy now collapsed, was a relief.

Until they got inside.

The thief had rifled through their things. Cabinets and drawers were open. The few articles of clothing they'd brought were thrown on the floor.

"It looks like our friend did a thorough job of looking for the ring," Michael said.

"Dear Lord, and I was probably out here, getting this—" she indicated the line that she hung over a hook in the wall "—while he was inside...."

Trying not to think too closely on the danger she might have been in, Flanna started picking up the strewn clothing.

"Obviously he didn't find it here, so why didn't he come out and finish the job?"

"He didn't want me to see his face." She pointed at the hooded mask on the floor. "In all this mess, he probably lost track of it."

Bracing herself for the jolt from the expected vision, Flanna retrieved the hooded mask left behind by the thief and concentrated on it. Her head went light and her surroundings receded.

He was grooming his horse—a black-and-white piebald with a black smudge running along the left cheek—and his brush strokes were as hard and firm as his angry tone. "I may be a thief, but I'm not a murderer!" He looked out past his horse to a lake. "My mistake that I missed the ring in the first place. I'll get it for you, and then we're through!"

Though she tried to keep the vision going, the emotional drop-off was like a break in reception. She'd seen what she was going to see and that was it.

Realizing Michael's gaze on her was intent, as if he were trying to get in her mind, she said, "He just was trying to steal the ring, like I said. He was the thief who broke in to my cottage." When he didn't speak, she said, "You can laugh now. Make fun of the poor deluded woman who thinks she has a gift for these things."

"Flanna…I'm sorry I hurt you."

He almost sounded as if he meant it. But it was too little, too late.

Wanting to distract him from taking the apology further, she said, "You're a mess, Michael Eagan. You should step into the shower and do something about that."

"I'll use all the water."

"Then we'll get more when we go into town," she said. "But you've got some scrapes that need cleaning. Go on with you now, and hand me your clothes so they're not a sodding mess." Nothing could stay dry in that small space if the shower was running. "When you're ready, I'll hand you clean clothes."

"If you insist."

"I do."

For once, Michael didn't argue, simply went into the minibathroom. She heard him thumping around as she finished picking up their things. A moment later, the door cracked open and a hand pushed out the filthy garments toward her like a peace offering. In taking them, she brushed her hand against his and a bolt of unwanted pleasure shot through her.

"Have a good shower," she mumbled, backing off.

One touch and he made her pulse race. Shaking her head, she found a bag for the dirty laundry. From the weight of his trousers, she realized he hadn't emptied the pockets, so she pulled out his wallet, cell phone and passport and placed them on the tiny countertop. And then she remembered the watch. She checked the other pocket. The moment her fingers touched the metal casing, they sizzled with a familiar current.

The pocket watch had something to show her, and she didn't even have time to prepare for it....

The alley bumped up along a brick building with a Guinness sign in front and a wall mural on the side advocating joining the two Irelands. From a back door came three men. Two looked around furtively, but the big one in front was looking down at something in his hand. Suddenly all three men went on alert and appeared ready to scatter.

"No!" screamed a male voice over rapid-fire gunshots.

The alley suddenly went cockeyed...half-focused...a dizzying, unsteady whirl... A man's chest exploded red as he collapsed on his back....

Gasping, Flanna grabbed onto the edge of the counter to steady herself. In the bathroom, the shower was running as hard as her heart. She felt as if she were invading Michael's privacy, but she couldn't stop now. Taking a shaky breath, she stared down into the cracked face of the watch and willed the vision back.

A second man fell forward on his face before he could use the gun in his hand. And a younger man, another gun drawn, got off a couple of shots before he, too, joined the others on the alley floor.

"No! No! No!"

Shaking hands picked up the discarded gun even as a vehicle zoomed off with a screech. The barrel of the gun

*whirled in a semicircle to follow the vehicle as if he meant to
use it, then, without going off, it dropped back to the pavement,
traded for a pocket watch as broken as the blood-covered man
who'd once owned it...*

A sob escaped Flanna and her knees gave way. Somehow,
with the watch still in hand, she got herself to a chair and sat.
For a moment, she couldn't think. The bloody image was so
clear in her mind that she couldn't get past it.

She'd been drawn in fully to Michael's memory, to his
seething, painful emotions.

After setting down the pocket watch, she stared at it
without touching it. Michael's father must have been the first
man to die. And the younger man...had that been the brother
he didn't want to talk about? The gun had been his.

Who carried a gun other than a policeman?

Living as she had in Ireland all her life, Flanna was no
stranger to this kind of violence. She suspected she knew
what she had seen.

The room shifted on her as if she were peering down a long
tunnel. Sounds became muffled and her head went light. No
wonder Michael hadn't wanted to talk about his father's and
brother's deaths. They'd died in what looked to be some kind
of Irish gang war. That's why he'd made those cryptic
comments that had led her to believe he had some kind of as-
sociation with criminals, might be one himself.

Had he been?

Was he?

Nearly choking on the thought, she didn't focus at first on
her name when Michael called to her.

"Flanna, those clothes?"

She came up out of the nightmare with her senses dulled.
Focusing seemed impossible. Michael was still in the bath-

room, his nude upper half hanging out the door. Heat shot through her, but she felt frozen.

"Flanna?" When she still didn't answer, he started out of the bathroom. "What's wrong?"

"Nothing," she lied, dropping her gaze so she wouldn't have to look at what she couldn't have. Even if Michael wanted her, she knew she had to stay away from him. They were wrong for each other. And after what she'd seen in her vision, how could she even trust him? "Go back in there. I'll be getting you those clothes now."

Flanna forced herself out of the chair. Forced herself to pick up the garments and bring them the several feet to the bathroom door, forced herself to hand them to Michael as if she hadn't had the vision.

The vision—should she tell him about it?

How could she? *Why* should she?

She'd asked him about his family and he'd kept it from her. Purposely, no doubt. Because he was ashamed or because he wasn't who he said he was?

No, surely that couldn't be right. Surely she would know if he was simply using her to get Caillech's treasures for himself.

Appalled at the thought that crawled into her mind, Flanna tried to shake it off. She reminded herself that Michael was a man with a mission, that he meant to bring a murderer to justice. She truly believed that.

Only, she couldn't have been more wrong about Erin. What if she were wrong again?

This time, at least, she couldn't use the excuse that she hadn't had a warning.

The bathroom door opened. "I'm decent and vacating the bathroom if you want to use it."

"I'm all right for the moment."

She wasn't, really, but what was she going to say? She couldn't tell him about her vision. At least not until she'd considered it further.

"We should report this incident to the authorities," Michael said.

"The *gardai* aren't going to be rushing out here in the middle of the night. And how do we explain what we're doing here? That we're not Travelers but pretending to be to catch a thief and murderer. If you insist on it, in the morning, we can go to the nearest *garda* station and make a report, but not every town has one, so first we'll have to find where to go."

"Then I'll call Murphy—"

"And tell him about the ring still in my possession? I'm sure he'll be full of sympathy, now won't he?"

"Well, when you put it that way..." Michael raked a hand through his wet hair. "We've gotten ourselves into quite a mess."

"I got us into this. I should have turned the ring over and let Murphy handle the investigation."

"You didn't rope me into anything, Flanna. I was determined to find the jewelry and the identity of the murderer myself. We'll think more clearly after we get some rest."

She couldn't help but note that he'd put the jewelry ahead of the murderer. "Take the bed, then."

"You mean sleep alone? You're not tired?" He gave her a closer look. "You've got to be exhausted."

Obviously he expected they would now sleep together after their bout of sex. Let him think she was still unhappy with him from earlier.

"I'm not ready for bed."

"Look, I can sleep outside again."

"No! It may not be safe." Just because some doubts had

risen in her mind didn't mean she wanted Michael taking even more chances because of her.

"I thought you said Joey the thief wasn't a murderer."

"I didn't mean him. I meant the one he's working for. The murderer. How do we know he's not around waiting for a chance at the ring? Just go to bed, Michael."

"But what about you?"

"I don't know that I'll be sleeping anytime soon. I'll alert you if I need the bed."

Michael stood there, staring at her for several moments as if he were trying to read her mind.

Too bad he wasn't psychic, she thought with irony.

Finally, he turned and headed for the alcove. Her heart in her throat, Flanna watched him climb into bed, not even turning away when he stretched out and groaned in pleasure and exhaustion.

He was asleep and snoring softly within moments.

After checking to be sure the trailer was locked up, Flanna found an extra pillow and blanket in the bench seat, which she would use as a makeshift bed. Thinking to get comfortable, if not actually sleep, she settled in and let exhaustion swallow her whole.

MICHAEL AWOKE disoriented. It took him a moment to remember where he was and whom he was with. Not that Flanna was in bed next to him. He sat up and looked through the kitchen area to find her fast asleep on the bench.

Purposely?

Even after the danger they'd shared, after she'd rescued him, she was too angry to sleep next to him?

It took him awhile and plenty of cold water splashed on his face to wake up fully. In the kitchen he found his wallet, passport, cell phone and pocket watch sitting on the counter. He slid them into his pockets and stared down at Flanna tucked under the blanket, her face smudged. Apparently she hadn't washed up, had gone right to bed despite her protests that she wasn't ready to sleep. Now, she made soft noises in her sleep, peacefully unaware of his presence.

Maybe that was the way things should remain between them.

So why did the thought put a knot in his gut?

Making as little noise as possible, he set about making coffee. He needed a clear head to face the day.

The tiny refrigerator produced several eggs and a slab of Irish bacon. He'd never made the fancy stuff in an Irish breakfast, but he could handle bacon and eggs. He pulled out a frying pan and laid out the bacon. Soon the narrow space filled with the combined scents of fresh coffee and sizzling bacon—smells mouth-watering enough to wake the near-dead.

Flanna shifted and groaned and opened her beautiful green eyes. "What are you about?"

"Making breakfast," he said, scrambling the eggs in a small bowl. "Not exactly an Irish breakfast, but it'll do. Go wash up if you want. Food will be on the table in about ten minutes."

Yawning, Flanna stood and headed for the small toilet, picking up the clean clothes as she went. She draped them on the door handle, then went inside.

Michael imagined her peeling off her dress and then her underthings. He imagined her naked. And when she turned on the shower, he imagined the water pounding her nude body, imagined her soaping her flesh, touching herself.

Enough imaginings.

He was hard-pressed not to join her, not to try to convince her that he'd been trying to ease the break between them. Then she would want to know why. How could he tell her about his past? She would see him as another mistake she'd made. Well, probably she already did. Better to keep things on an even keel between them. Soon he would be gone from here and she could forget him.

Very soon, he hoped, now regretting the danger he'd brought to this woman that he would never forget.

"I'M LOOKING FOR my brother, Joey," Flanna told the Traveler woman who was washing some clothing in a stream. "He has dark hair and wears the stallion tattoo on his upper arm. He has one of those old horse-drawn caravans. I thought he might come by here to give his horse a drink."

"You talking about Joseph Begley?"

"That would be him!" Flanna said excitedly. "So you know Joey?"

"Not know him. But we met up with him yesterday for a while," the woman said. "A couple of miles from here."

A couple of miles... It might as well have been a hundred.

Still, she asked, "What road was he camped on? Maybe I can catch up to him."

The woman gave her an intent look and said, "Don't remember," and went back to her laundry.

She was lying; Flanna was certain of it. She was equally certain she wasn't going to get another thing out of the close-mouthed Traveler. But at least she had gotten something. A last name. A detail that didn't excite Michael nearly as much as it did her.

And so it went, them circling and crossing roads they'd already been over. Another day hurtling by without their catching up to the thief.

"We need to stop for gas," Michael said. "Um, fuel. Petrol."

"Fine. I could use a leg stretch. And we could pick up something to eat."

The next town held a petrol station with a minimart. Michael stayed with the vehicle, while Flanna went inside and quickly filled a basket. At the counter, she picked up a newspaper that covered county news, wondering if she would find a story about her and Michael being named fugitives from the law. At least they hadn't made the front page.

It was a soft day, rain coming down light but steady. So rather than having a picnic, they pulled to the side of the road and ate in the cab of the truck. For once not having much of an appetite, Flanna took a few bites of her sandwich, then traded her food for the newspaper. A follow-up blurb on Bridget Rafferty's murder was all she could find related to the investigation. No mention of her or of Michael.

About to fold up the paper, she caught an advertisement for Clondowney Golf and Country Club, particularly the green shield with the red flag that was its insignia.

"There it is, then, the shield with the flag inside. That's where I've seen it before!"

"Seen what?"

"Remember I told you about the insignia on the glove? I saw it in two different visions, the first being when Bridget was killed. The hand holding the candlestick was gloved, and the glove bore that insignia."

"I remember your telling me."

Was that his way of sharing his disbelief?

Flanna clenched her jaw to keep from telling him what she'd seen by touching his pocket watch. Perhaps that would convince him, but she didn't want to bring up his past. She'd felt the depth of his emotions and she didn't want to be the cause of stirring up those old feelings. And she was still a bit uneasy thinking he might have more of a personal interest in this case than he'd let on.

"The killer belongs to the Clondowney Golf and Country Club along the coast not far from the cliffs of Moher," she said. "I wonder if the Rafferty brothers are among the members."

"Something to look into when we get back."

Flanna couldn't tell if he was serious or if he was just trying to pacify her. She was glad when he finished his lunch and they were off on their journey again. The hunt for the thief might be frustrating, but at least she felt good about learning something that might be of use in unearthing a murderer.

They were exploring yet another country road, when Flanna looked out to the lake and realized she'd seen it before. Not on the road but in her vision.

"Wait. He was here. I saw this lake when I touched the hood last night." She rolled down the window and stuck out her head to get a better look. A staked horse grazed—the same piebald Cobb that had been in her vision. "Pull over, Michael. Hurry!"

Without comment he did as she demanded.

Flanna threw open the door and got out.

"What are you doing? Flanna!"

Nothing was going to stop her. She swiftly circled trees that went almost to the edge of the lake, and as she drew closer to the horse, the caravan came into view. The wagon seemed deserted. She went straight for it, ignoring Michael's command to stop and wait for him.

She was almost to the caravan before she realized her mistake. Heart pounding, she tried to dodge the man who came at her from behind the wagon, but he was faster and stronger than she.

He grabbed her, whipped her around and shouted to Michael, "Stop if you want her to live."

Chapter Fourteen

Michael's heart nearly stopped. Fearing for Flanna, he stopped dead in his tracks.

"He won't hurt me, Michael," she said with more confidence than he was feeling. "He's not a murderer."

"How do you know what I am or am not?" Begley asked.

"I'm a *bean feasa*," Flanna pronounced, as if that would impress him. "How do you think we found you, Joseph Begley? I saw this camp—you grooming your piebald—in a vision."

What in the world was she doing? Michael wondered. Now she was taking on her grandmother's persona? Did she really think she could talk the thief in to cooperating?

He stepped forward, but Begley tightened his hold on Flanna's waist, bringing her up off her feet.

"Siobhan!" he yelled, never taking his eyes off Michael. "Get out here and hook up the horse to the caravan!"

A muffled response from the wagon was followed by a dark-haired young woman in a red tank top and cropped black leggings coming out to see what was happening.

"Joey!" she said with a gasp, then clambered down to do as the man ordered.

"The woman is correct in that I'm not one for violence," Begley said. "Unless I need to be."

With that, he used his free hand to produce a knife, which he held to Flanna's throat. Michael froze, rooted to the spot lest the other man use it on the woman he loved. He said a quick prayer—for her safety and for the know-how to keep her from harm.

"Don't do anything foolish, Begley. You say Flanna is correct. That means so far you're only guilty of breaking in to her cottage and stealing Bridget Rafferty's jewelry. You didn't have anything to do with the murders."

"Aye," Flanna said. "The authorities will go easy on you if you cooperate and lead them to the killer."

"The two of you are the ones who need to cooperate." Without allowing his gaze to waver, he called to Siobhan. "Are we hooked up yet?"

"Just about."

"You'll take the reins."

Begley backed up toward the caravan, keeping Flanna in front of him like a shield. Michael couldn't get to the other man, not with Flanna as a target in between.

"What are you doing?" Michael asked.

"Making sure you don't follow me if you want to see your woman alive. If you stay back, I'll drop her off in a town a ways from here and she can contact you to come get her."

His woman…she was in his heart if not in fact. The idea of losing Flanna tied a knot in his stomach.

"You won't hurt her?"

"Not if you don't interfere."

Not that Michael would actually trust Begley to keep to his word. Besides which, the thief still wanted the ring, and Flanna had it on her.

What were his choices, though? If he acted, Begley could be unpredictable.

On the other side of the caravan, Siobhan climbed up into the driver's seat and grabbed the reins with both hands. "Let's go, Joey. Now!"

Slowly moving forward, Michael watched for an opening that didn't involve the knife blade slashing across Flanna's throat.

He met her gaze and his mouth went dry. Her determination to escape the situation was palpable. He could see it in her eyes. Silently he tried telling her not to act foolishly, but he knew she would ignore him if she thought she had a chance.

When Begley reached out his hand for a means to haul them on board the caravan, Flanna took advantage of the moment's distraction. Her hand came up and she dug her fingers into his soft underarm flesh so that Begley yowled in surprise and let go of the knife. Even as it clattered to the boards below the seat, Michael sprang toward them.

Yelling something Michael didn't understand, Begley literally threw Flanna at him and jumped on board. Michael caught her, but they went down together as Siobhan slapped the reins to make the piebald move off.

"Don't let him get away!" Flanna yelled, scrambling to the side out of his way.

Seeing that she was all right, Michael went after the caravan on foot. The horse picked up speed, but so did he. And before Siobhan could turn them out of the grassy area onto the road, Michael gripped a handhold on the side of the wagon. With a burst of speed, he thrust himself forward. Begley turned in his seat toward the new threat, but wasn't quite ready for the attack.

"C'mon down, you bastard!" Michael grabbed him by the front of his shirt and got a secure grip, then let go of the wagon so they both catapulted to the ground.

"Joey!" Siobhan's scream was followed by the sound of the horse and caravan being pulled to a stop.

Michael rolled with the thief, trading punches and vying for the upper hand. Begley's fist jammed into his nose and mouth, and sharp pain accompanied a spurt of blood on Michael's face. Begley freed himself, but Michael caught onto his leg and twisted, flipping the thief onto his back.

He pounced and, with a knee in Begley's chest, got off one good punch that knocked the thief senseless.

"Flanna, get the nylon line!" he yelled.

As she ran to the trailer, Siobhan jumped from the caravan, yelling, "Joey, are you all right?"

The thief merely groaned in return.

Still with a knee at Begley's sternum, Michael thought the woman looked as if she were ready to jump him and so put out a hand to stop her. "Stay back if you don't want him to hurt even more."

"Joey? What should I do?"

"Get out. Go!"

"It'll go better on you if you stay and cooperate with the cops," Michael said, then corrected himself. "The *gardai*."

The woman looked ready to panic, but she didn't run. "I'm not leaving you, Joey."

True love, Michael thought. She was going to stand by her man, no matter what.

Returning from the trailer with the canopy line, Flanna kept a wary eye on the other woman. Michael took it from her and quickly secured Begley's hands behind his back, then attached the line to his feet, as well. The thief wasn't going anywhere, not until Michael was through with him.

"Where is the Rafferty woman's jewelry?" he asked.

"I don't know what you're talking about."

"It'll go easier on you if you do. Bridget Rafferty was murdered."

"I'm no murderer!"

"You're an accessory."

"He's not!" Siobhan said. "He wasn't hired to do anything until *after* the woman was dead."

"Siobhan, keep your mouth shut!"

"No, I won't! Do you want to be arrested for something you didn't do, Joseph Begley?" Siobhan turned to Michael. "Joey had nothing to do with the Rafferty woman's murder, I swear!"

"Who did then?"

Her dark eyes filled with tears. "I don't know."

"It's up to you, then, Begley," Michael said.

With a groan, Begley gave over. "All right. I was hired to rob the cottage and I turned over the jewelry the next morning. I had nothing to do with any murder."

"Who hired you?"

"He introduced himself as Paddy O'Bannon, but a smart man wouldn't go looking for him under that name."

"What did he look like?"

"Taller than me, but other than that, I couldn't really tell you. We met at night, and he wore a trench coat and a hat that hid his face, so I never really saw it."

Taking out his cell phone, Michael said, "I'm going to call Detective Garda Kevin Murphy, who is in charge of the case. You can try to convince him of that."

"And you can try to convince him that Flanna McKenna hasn't stolen the Rafferty woman's ring!"

"I haven't stolen it," Flanna said, then turned to Michael. "Call Murphy. I'll explain everything."

That's what Michael feared. Either Murphy would lock her up for a thief or he would lock her away in an asylum.

But what else was there to do? Begley might tell the truth about Flanna's having the ring, but that didn't mean they could let him go.

Michael pulled out his cell phone and made the call.

"I SHOULD LOCK YOU both up," Murphy said after interrogating Joseph Begley and having a guard escort him to his cell.

Begley hadn't come up with any more information for them other than the make of the car his contact drove—a black Mercedes.

"If you're going to take action against anyone, it should be me alone," Flanna said, swallowing the lump in her throat. The pouch containing the ring secured to the inside of her dress pressed against her flesh, a physical reminder of what had put in motion the series of events that had landed them here. "I'm the one who kept back the ring after the theft."

"I knew about it and didn't make her give it over." Michael covered her hand with his, making her catch her breath. "We're in this together."

They were alone with Murphy in the interrogation room. The detective drummed his fingers against the table as if that would help him think. The sound rattled along Flanna's spine as she waited for his verdict.

"Your tracking down Begley and calling me to come get him is the only reason I'll be giving you both the benefit of the doubt. Convince me as to why I shouldn't arrest you."

Flanna realized she had to tell the detective the truth, no matter that he might not believe her. "I thought the ring would lead me to the rest of Caillech's treasures."

"Lead you how?"

She hesitated only a second before saying, "Psychically."

"Well, now…" Murphy got that look of disbelief on his

face that Flanna so dreaded. "So you're saying the ring gave you some kind of vision to track down its mates?"

"Not exactly. I had visions from the different pieces of jewelry, yes, but not like that. They were cursed by the original owner, however, and linked forever by Caillech's curse. I thought that if we got closer to the other pieces…"

"The ring would alert you?"

"Aye. Something like that."

Murphy shook his head. "I've heard a lot of stories in my day, but yours is pure blarney if I ever heard it."

"'Tis nothing but the truth!" Flanna said hotly. "And your disbelief is why I didn't tell you everything in the first place—"

"Here's another truth," Michael interrupted. "Flanna was never paid for her work. The contract says she's supposed to be paid when she turns over the remaining pieces and copies—remember that Bridget gave them over to her willingly—but Barry Rafferty vowed he would never pay her. So if you care to use that fact in Flanna's behalf, there's some wiggle room as to the status of the ring."

"Wiggle room. You sound more like a solicitor than a private investigator."

Thinking Michael sounded like a man who knew how to talk his way out of difficult situations, Flanna remembered her vision when touching the pocket watch. Glancing at him now, at his face bruised and swollen from his fight with Joseph Begley, remembering that he'd been the one to call in Murphy, she felt ashamed that she'd suspected his motives in wanting to catch up to the thief.

Flanna now realized it had been her way of keeping Michael at a distance, to prove to herself that her romantic inheritance was merely a pretty wish. She'd spent years not wanting to believe in the McKenna Legacy, and the vision had given her an excuse to prove her old self correct.

She'd been wrong, but so had Michael.

Why couldn't he have told her about his past?

She'd asked him directly about his family and he'd avoided the truth, whatever that was, which made unconditional trust a bit difficult for her.

"Let's say I give you the benefit of the doubt," Murphy said, interrupting her thoughts. "You'll turn over the ring now?"

"But I haven't found its mates! We haven't yet flushed out the murderer!"

"And just how do you intend to do that?"

She'd been thinking on it for some time now. "What if another piece of the collection is found?"

"Are there more pieces than we already know about?" Murphy asked.

"Not likely. But I can lie." She was getting good at that. "What if I put out the word that I found another heretofore missing piece of the collection from some obscure source who is willing to sell to the highest bidder? We can give a party where I offer it for sale by public auction. That would surely bring out the collectors, including the person behind the thefts and murders."

"How do you plan to attract prospective buyers without actually having anything to sell?" Murphy asked.

"Oh, but I will have something—a piece in a case, unavailable for closer inspection until the night of the auction. I've made enough copies of the collection that I can use the design to create one additional piece to look like it was done by the original designer."

"Flanna, surely you can't mean to set yourself up as a

target again," Michael protested. "You've been through enough in these past few days."

"It may be the only way to draw out the killer."

"How do you even know he's still in the vicinity?" Murphy asked.

"Because I still have the ring," Flanna reminded him. "This man has killed three women to get the whole collection and isn't likely to stop now. Whether or not you believe the curse and the prediction that the wearer can obtain Caillech's power on Beltane, I would say the killer does and will be desperate to complete the suite. Also, the killer obviously belongs to the Clondowney Golf and Country Club, which means it's someone who lives in one of the nearby towns if not in Killarra itself."

"What's this about Clondowney?" Murphy asked.

"The killer wore leather gloves with an insignia at the wrist. A green shield with a red flag inside. It took me days to place where I'd seen it before."

Murphy started. "That's Clondowney's symbol."

"Exactly."

"If you're right, the killer belongs to the golf club."

"A member who drives a black Mercedes," Michael added.

"There was a black Mercedes parked nearby in Ballyloy when we stopped at the mart and I went inside to get information about Begley," Flanna said. "The moment I seemed to note the vehicle, it drove off. Now I'm wondering if the killer was behind the wheel."

"He could have been tracking us," Michael said, "while making sure Begley stayed out of our way."

Flanna looked at Murphy. "Surely you can do something with that information about the vehicle."

"I can look in to the records, make a list of any member

who drives such a vehicle," the detective agreed. "That should narrow it down somewhat."

"There was a black Mercedes parked in front of Rafferty Manor," Michael said. "And it's a sure bet the Rafferty boys belong to Clondowney."

"I imagine many other members of the club from other towns drive a Mercedes," Murphy said, obviously not wanting it to be one of their own. "And while I'm at it, I'll do a search on the name Begley gave us just in case it leads somewhere." He consulted his notes. "That would be one Paddy O'Bannon."

"What about my plan?" Flanna asked. It sounded like Murphy was being agreeable. "Are we set then?"

"I don't like it," Michael said. "And I'm sure Detective Murphy doesn't, either."

"He's correct. You really should stay out of this, Miss McKenna."

"I know that's your official position."

"It has to be. You never should have involved yourself in the first place."

"But I did. *We* did," she said, including Michael. So the detective wasn't on board with her plan, after all. Telling herself not to panic, she reminded him, "You wouldn't have Begley now if we hadn't interfered."

"True, but—"

"But should I 'find' this new piece of the collection, you wouldn't stop me from bringing it to everyone's attention, now, would you?"

Murphy fixed his gaze on her for a moment, then shook his head. "It's a stubborn woman you are, Flanna McKenna."

"I simply want the murders to stop. There'll be more if we don't end this soon," she predicted.

"And you may be the next victim," Michael said.

"Not with you to watch my back." Flanna looked from him to Murphy. "Well?"

"I can't stop you from having an auction."

"And you'll let me keep possession of the ring?"

"For now," Murphy agreed. "Not because I believe it has some magical power, but because our killer might believe it, as you said. Plus, your partner here had a point about your rights to hang onto the ring until you're paid for your work. As long as you keep me informed of every move you make from now on, I won't interfere."

Breathing a sigh of relief, Flanna said, "Agreed."

They left the station and started on their way back to the cottage on foot.

"This plan of yours is dangerous," Michael said.

"But it might just be the thing." She wanted to tell him that should the killer have any part of the collection on him, the ring would warn her. But he would simply scoff. "It's worth the risk, Michael, isn't it? To stop a killer from striking again?"

Should the killer put the entire suite together in time for the Beltane deadline, he would then have Caillech's power. Two warped minds together…and the power to wreak who knew what kind of havoc.

Another fear she couldn't share.

Flanna looked up to see Eamon Rafferty coming down the street toward them, a scowl set on his florid face. She tensed but felt Michael's hand go around her waist in support.

"I need to speak with you," Eamon said directly to her.

"There's nothing I can tell you—"

"You don't understand. It's me who needs to do the talking. You are owed an apology, Miss McKenna. I know I was harsh at the cemetery, but I was very upset, having just buried my mother and all."

An apology? Surprised, she said, "Apology accepted," and tried to move on.

"Wait. Barry can be…harsh. It was wrong of him to blame you for Mother's death and for the theft of her jewelry and the copies. You shall get everything you deserve. I'll see to it myself. Good day."

Left speechless, Flanna watched Eamon Rafferty walk to his car and drive away.

"Did you believe a word of that?" Michael asked.

"You didn't?"

"It's awfully convenient, don't you think, that he happened to run in to us right from the *garda* station?"

"He sounded sincere. And it has been Barry who's been so awful."

"Don't underestimate him."

"All right, I won't."

If Eamon showed up at the auction, she would have more reason to suspect him. Then, again, she guessed she would have to suspect every person who showed. She only wished Michael had offered her some support.

This plan of hers had to work. If it did, she would target the killer, stop him from getting Caillech's power, end the murders and find justice for Bridget and the other two murder victims.

And then, when all was said and done, the man she loved would be free to return to America, and her gran's legacy would be lost to her forever.

Chapter Fifteen

Luckily, Flanna had kept her casting forms from the copies she'd made for Bridget. Michael shook his head at how complicated this jewelry-making business was. Flanna told him how she produced the mold from the original, injected liquid wax, which, when cooled, would leave a hardened wax piece identical to the original and then made the casting form. From that, the wax was burned out in a kiln, and finally, molten metal was poured. He saw her being able to skip the first several steps as a huge time-saver.

While he paced and worried for Flanna, he went over every detail of all they'd learned, and then planned and plotted for the coming days. Finally, in the early hours of the morning, he fell asleep.

Waking a bit after dawn, Michael found Flanna had gone to her bed at last, fully clothed. Though he tried to move around the living room quietly, she woke and immediately went to work. She took the cast piece from the kiln and with hand tools, smoothed out the tiny openings in the design. She went strong all morning, stopping only to eat something when he insisted.

All the while he thought about Flanna's safety, or lack thereof. His being around didn't guarantee anything. Only by luck had she come through their charade without being hurt or killed. If something had happened to her, he would have blamed himself. Something could still happen to her. She was making herself a target.

"You don't have to go through with this," Michael said when Flanna stopped for a tea break.

"You're wrong. I do. Act selflessly in another's behalf— that's part of Gran's legacy to us."

"I thought you didn't believe in the legacy."

"I've changed my mind, Michael." Her expression and voice softened. "At least I want to believe. I've come to realize that a person can't just be alone in life and can't act only for one's self. I need to do this. I need to find justice for Bridget. That's part of my inheritance. Gran would expect nothing less of me."

"She expects more *for* you," Michael said, drawing closer so that he was engaged by her very presence. For a small woman, she made a large impact. She filled all his empty spaces. "What about the rest? The love part?"

He met her gaze and saw a longing that touched him. He felt it, too. Felt the sadness of knowing what he wanted. What he couldn't have. He couldn't tell Flanna about his past…and he couldn't have her if he didn't. She hated the lies she'd been forced to tell as part of their charade of a marriage. He knew that. His not telling her was simply another lie. Eventually she would learn the truth, and when she did, her soft expression would turn hard when she looked at him.

When she judged him.

Finally she sipped from her mug, then said, "If it's meant to be, then I'll accept whatever life has to offer."

Meant to be…with another man. The thought ripped up Michael inside.

Though Flanna went back to work, it looked to him as if the piece was almost complete.

"About this party," he said. "I assume you have a plan."

"I do. Later today I'm going to see Lisa Madden about helping me."

"You're going to tell her the truth?"

"Of course not. The truth is between you and me and Murphy. But I need to get the word out. Lisa Madden knows everyone who is anyone in this part of the country. And I need a grand place to hold the party. I was thinking Saturday night at the Clondowney Golf and Country Club would be the perfect time and place."

"Saturday—Beltane."

"Yes."

He nodded and thought for a moment, then said, "But you're not a member of Clondowney."

"Lisa may be, though. I remember Bridget telling me they were going to the club for lunch. Even if Lisa was Bridget's guest, she would probably know what we have to do, who we might have to ask, to hold an event there."

"We?"

Flanna looked as if she couldn't breathe. "Frankly, Michael, I need your cooperation and your client's money. I wouldn't ask you, but I'm broke. I can't hold an event there on my own."

Remembering she hadn't been paid for several months work, he said, "Money's not a problem." He would pay for the event himself if necessary. He wasn't going to let her do this alone. He was going to protect her with his life.

She let go of the breath and her shoulders sagged. "Good. Good."

Back to work she went for another round, using hand tools

to finish filing out the inside of the knots, to sand down the edges on a rubber grinding wheel, then to polish and round the edges of the piece, giving it a tridimensional look.

"It's ready to cook again," she said, placing the piece in her kiln. "And I'm ready to talk to Lisa Madden. After I shower and change, of course."

"I'll go with you."

Flanna shook her head. "You have to stay and make sure no one gets in here. We can't chance someone stumbling onto the truth."

As much as he hated letting her go anywhere alone, he agreed with her about protecting their secret. If anyone found out about her making a fake addition to the collection, they were through. It wasn't as if he had nothing to do, after all. He had people to call and plans to make.

Certain that she would succeed in arranging to hold the auction at the golf club Saturday night, he didn't have much time to set up the proper security team. First he would call his own agency and get a list of referrals here in Ireland. Then he would alert his contact at Interpol.

Whatever materialized, or didn't, between Flanna and him, he wouldn't let anything happen to the woman he loved.

FLANNA WAS SURE to keep an eye out for any sign of trouble as she went in search of Lisa Madden. Driving, she constantly checked her side- and rearview mirrors to make certain that no one was following.

No sign of a black Mercedes.

Unfortunately, when she arrived at Madden Interiors, there was no sign of Lisa, either.

"You might be finding her at Antique Heaven," Lisa's assistant told her when Flanna insisted she had to find the woman immediately. "Then again, she could be at one of the other dozen antique shops in the area. She's redoing the front parlor at the Crawford estate and is on the hunt for period pieces."

Flanna thanked the pretty redhead and set off. How foolish of her to think this would be easy. No matter the hurdle, however, she would handle it.

The owner of Antique Heaven told her Lisa had left a half hour before and was headed for Ye Olde Antique Shoppe in a neighboring town. Flanna spent barely a moment wondering if she should wait for Lisa to return to her shop before setting off in pursuit of the woman.

The drive gave her time to think about Michael, and about how, if her plan worked to draw out the killer, he would be leaving Ireland soon. The thought left an empty spot inside her—more like a chasm, really—and she wondered how this could have happened when she'd so carefully guarded her heart all these years. Erin Cassidy had left her immune to romantic notions. Or so she'd thought. It had simply taken the right man to break through her defenses.

Or the wrong man, Flanna thought, heartsick knowing this to be the case.

While Michael brought out both her soft and wild sides, she longed for something more substantial from him. For his respect, his acknowledgment of her gift. For his faith in her that he could tell her things about his shadowy past that perhaps he couldn't speak of with anyone else. If a relationship wasn't built on truth and trust, then it was doomed from the start.

So why didn't she want to admit that? Why the hope that it could still work out?

She was still trying to swallow her mixed feelings for Michael when, twenty minutes later, she found a place to park down the street from the referenced antique shop. About to leave the car, she spotted Lisa standing on a side street nowhere near the shop. And Lisa was not alone.

From their dark expressions, Lisa and Hugh Nolan, the Raffertys' houseman, were arguing about something. Flanna thought it odd that they knew each other well enough to argue at all. At Rafferty Manor, Hugh had barely nodded politely to Lisa the few times Flanna had seen her there. Thinking it had something to do with Bridget's death, or perhaps the Rafferty sons, Flanna sat frozen in the car, reluctant to interrupt.

Several minutes went by before the argument abruptly ended and Hugh stalked off down the main street, away from Flanna, never glancing back. Lisa stared after Hugh as he got in to his car and drove out of town.

Still Flanna waited and wondered what she had just witnessed. Something kept her from leaving the car and announcing her presence.

Eventually, Lisa crossed the street and Flanna realized she was going into the antique shop. So had she been in town for a full half hour—the head start she'd had on Flanna—without attending to business? Surely Lisa hadn't been arguing with Hugh that whole time.

Flanna stayed put for another ten minutes before leaving the car and heading for the shop. Opening the door, she came face-to-face with Lisa, who was just leaving.

"Flanna McKenna, whatever are you doing here?" Though she quickly veiled her surprised expression, Lisa didn't sound pleased.

"I was looking for you," Flanna said, giving the other woman a sunny smile meant to reassure her. "Your assistant told me you were at Antique Heaven and the owner there said you might be here, and so here I am."

"You're following me? Whatever for?"

Was Lisa irritated at being followed or because she feared she'd been seen arguing with Hugh?

Playing innocent, as if she had just arrived on the scene, Flanna said, "Sorry if I'm inconveniencing you, but I really need your help. Is there somewhere to get a cuppa where we can talk in private?"

Luckily there was a tea room at the opposite end of the block. Lisa led the way, her posture stiff, but by the time they got inside, she was acting more like her friendly self.

Flanna waited until they were seated and had given their orders before asking, "Are you by any chance a member of Clondowney Golf and Country Club?"

"Yes, of course, I need to be for my interior design business. I've met many of my clients there or through other members."

"I thought that might be the case."

Lisa frowned. "Are you looking for new clients, as well? I could introduce you to several women who might be interested in your original designs. Were you looking for an invite for lunch or something?"

"Or something. Actually, I was hoping to hold a function there on Saturday night."

"Function?"

"An auction. While I was away for the last few days, I followed a lead about a piece of jewelry." Not too much of a lie, Flanna thought. "It panned out and I made a deal with the owner. I agreed to sell it for him. At auction."

"Auction? What was the find?"

"The last piece of Caillech's collection."

Lisa frowned. "But I thought Bridget had all but two—the pieces stolen from the murdered women in Boston and London. It isn't one of those, is it?"

"No, of course not," Flanna assured her.

Lisa of course wouldn't want to be involved if she thought everything wasn't on the up-and-up.

"Then where did this mysterious piece come from?"

"Actually, I had heard rumors of a second pendant ever since getting involved with Bridget. This was said to be a bit more elaborate than the first, with a much larger cabochon. I was trying to track the piece down for Bridget. One of my sources finally came through for me," she said, her smile ironic. "After reading about the deaths associated with the collection, the owner is willing to sell and to give me a handsome commission, which I sorely need since Barry Rafferty doesn't seem inclined to pay me for the work I did for his mother."

Lisa didn't say anything; she seemed mired in contemplation. Flanna chose to give her a few minutes when the tea and scones arrived.

She'd just slathered her first scone with strawberry jam and clotted cream when Lisa said, "So you want me to arrange a room at the club. And, I assume, refreshments."

"Aye. And I was hoping you could get the word out to the right people to help generate interest."

"For Saturday—you do mean tomorrow night?"

"The sooner the better, wouldn't you agree?"

"Considering how much trouble the collection has been to the women who have had the pieces in their possession…"

"Trust me, I have no plans to wear the pendant and invoke the curse."

Though she hated having to embellish her lies, Flanna kept up the pretense to convince Lisa that she truly had what she claimed to have.

"Your not trying on the originals hasn't kept you safe," Lisa said, stirring sugar and milk into her tea. "How many more attacks can you survive without being seriously hurt?"

Of course Lisa knew about the attack associated with the robbery at the cottage…but she had said it as if she knew there had been more than one incident.

Before Flanna could ask about it, Lisa said, "Word is going around town about you and Michael being attacked in some castle ruins a few days ago."

Flanna settled down inside and took that bite of her scone, which, unfortunately, with the turn of conversation, seemed tasteless. It had been nearly twenty-four hours since they'd given Murphy all the details. Killarra was a small town. Bridget Rafferty's murder was still on everyone's minds. Of course the word about anything involving the case surrounding it would already be spreading.

She said, "Then you know Michael caught the man who attacked us—a Traveler named Joseph Begley—and he's now in custody. He's the thief who broke in to the cottage and stole the remainder of Bridget's collection, as well."

"I thought that was Sean Hogan."

Flanna shook her head. "Hogan was set up, as was I. Now the authorities believe that, as well."

"So the authorities have the murderer."

"No," Flanna said. "Only one of the thieves."

Lisa frowned. "This is all so confusing…and disturbing."

"I agree. That's why I'm in such a hurry to get rid of the pendant. I want my money so I can leave and go back to my real life and forget the last months."

"And of course I'll help you do that. Bridget, bless her soul, would have wanted me to help you in any way I could." Taking a sip of her tea, Lisa shook her head. "She would be so ashamed of her sons."

"Did one of them do something awful while we were gone?"

"It's just the way they've been acting…the feeling I've had

about how they're handling this whole situation. They both need money, and it occurred to me…" Lisa suddenly stopped and looked uncomfortable. "I shouldn't talk out of turn."

"You think one of them might be guilty?"

Lisa overcame her momentary embarrassment. She nodded. "Or both of them together."

"Two men plotting to kill their own mother?"

"Not necessarily. Bridget wasn't supposed to be home that night."

Flanna remembered her vision and Bridget's reaction when she realized she was being robbed. The woman had not only known her killer, but she'd also been hurt by his actions.

"I hope I'm wrong, for Bridget's sake," Lisa said.

"I hope we're both wrong."

Avoiding further speculation, they turned their attention to their tea and scones and talked instead about what Flanna needed to make the auction a success. Then Lisa made a call to the club and learned that all the common spaces were spoken for. She did arrange to rent one of the luxury suites in the annex, however.

"Not a bad idea," Lisa said. "We can arrive early, make sure everything is set up, then relax for a while before getting ready for the party. The suite has several bedrooms."

"Perfect," Flanna said, smiling. Underneath, however, she was already worrying how this would play out.

People would come out of curiosity, of course, but would the killer? She was counting on it. How could someone go to such lengths and not be tempted by the final piece of the collection?

Final two pieces, she reminded herself. She still had the original ring and the killer knew it.

Though Michael was arranging for the best in security, Flanna couldn't rid herself of the notion that she was once more putting herself in terrible danger.

Chapter Sixteen

Lisa suggested they drive to Clondowney to check out the facilities in person. Flanna agreed. The idea was a sound one and she would have a better idea of what Michael would need to watch for in the way of security. She wondered if the murderer would actually try to steal the pendant rather than just make a bid for it.

The annex was isolated from the main club building on the other side of the golf course and backed cliffs that plunged down several hundred feet to the Atlantic. Flanna stood at the edge and stared down at the foam made by the sea crashing into boulders at the foot of the cliffs. Though normally not afraid of heights, she felt her chest tighten and her pulse rush as hard as the crashing waves below.

She was grateful when the events coordinator suggested they proceed to the inside of the facility.

"You'll have the entire first floor."

He led them inside a huge parlor with enough couches and chairs for at least a dozen people, then into a dining room with an equal amount of seating, as well as a complete kitchen. Five bedrooms and a smaller parlor on the other side of the building completed the suite.

The place was downright cavernous compared to the

cottage and especially compared to her Dublin flat. Flanna explored one of the bedrooms and found a door that opened to the outside.

"All bedrooms and both parlors have exterior doors, of course," the events coordinator said.

Easy egress for a thief, Flanna thought as she nodded and smiled at the man.

But how would a thief actually get to the pendant in the midst of all the potential buyers? Not only would it be in a secured case, but there would be security men working the party, as well. It would have to be isolated, away from the main gathering.

In one of the bedrooms complete with escape route...

"Now, let's have a look at the suggested menu."

A half hour later, after the events coordinator reassured her he would send out an e-mail notifying every member of her auction, Lisa said she, too, would put the word out through her client list.

"If you like," she added, "I can come early and help you make sure everything is ready before the guests arrive."

"Would you? You can even have one of the bedrooms if you want to change clothes or rest."

"Perfect."

Flanna thanked Lisa profusely for all her help, then drove straight to Shannon alone.

Needing a dress and shoes not only suitable for the occasion but also symbolic as well, she figured the city was her best bet. Indeed, she found what she needed without a lot of fuss. After grabbing some take-away, she headed back to Killarra, eating while she drove.

Still, by the time she returned to the cottage, the sun had already set. Exhausted, Flanna stood in front of her door, juggling her packages while sorting keys on her ring.

"Excuse me, but I need to see your identification."

Startled at the sudden appearance of a man wearing dark pants and a pullover, Flanna jumped back, her pulse racing. "And who would you be?"

"Security."

"And *your* identification?" she asked, ready to run if he couldn't produce it.

But produce it he did. Relieved, Flanna did the same.

"Sorry, Miss McKenna, but Mr. Eagan would have had my head if I'd let anyone inside without checking first."

"Of course. Where is Mr. Eagan?"

"Looking for you. He expected you back hours ago. He, um, said you didn't own a cell phone."

Flanna rolled her eyes and unlocked the door. Michael had probably *said* more than that; he'd probably cursed the fact. Considering the circumstances, she probably should have gotten one in the last week, but it was a bit late for that regret.

"You'd better call Mr. Eagan, then, and let him know I'm all right."

Something she might have done herself earlier, she supposed, but Flanna had known Michael would object to her going anywhere alone other than into town. He would have insisted on coming with her while the pendant was cooking in the kiln. As it was, she hadn't expected him to leave the cottage in search of her whereabouts, though at least he'd waited to do so until there was someone else to guard the place.

She checked the piece she'd left to cook in the kiln. The metal was cool and ready to be pickled, brushed and polished.

She'd hung up the new dress and had started to change when the phone rang.

Michael!

Heart thumping, she picked up the phone and said, "Look, I'm sorry I didn't call to let you know where I was all day."

"I'm not a mind reader, you know" came an amused female voice.

"Keelin!"

Relieved she didn't have to deal with Michael just yet, Flanna threw herself across the bed to talk to her sister. And then it hit her that they'd just spoken a few days before.

"Is this a social call, I hope?" The hesitation at the other end sent a chill right through her. Her sister had seen something. "Keelin, talk to me."

"It's not good."

That statement meant Keelin had indeed dreamed through her eyes again, had seen something bad coming. "Tell me."

Her sister saying "I saw a cliff" was no surprise. "You were struggling…looking down at a sickening drop…fighting to stay on your feet."

Remembering the unusually queasy feeling she'd had looking down at the waves, Flanna choked out, "Did I? Stay on my feet, I mean?"

"I don't know. I woke up."

She had that uneasy feeling again just thinking about the drop off the cliff. "Thanks for warning me."

"So it hasn't happened yet?"

"Tomorrow…"

"Flanna, don't go there, wherever it is."

"I have no choice. If I don't…" Flanna quickly brought Keelin up to speed on what had gone on since they'd spoken on her birthday, ending with the proposed auction for the fake pendant. "I want to stop the killer before there's another victim."

"I don't want that victim to be you."

"It won't be, Keelin, really. Now that you've told me about

your dream, I'll be doubly on my guard. And Michael is providing top-notch security."

"Michael. The way you say his name...he is the one, then? Gran's legacy?"

Flanna laughed. "Michael doesn't believe in legacies. And while he might share other things, he doesn't share the truth. Not the hard truth."

"Sounds complicated."

"Too complicated."

"Anything worth having is worth fighting for. If you have feelings for him, then you must fight for him, Flanna."

"I did that once before."

"But that was Erin and this is Michael and they sound nothing alike."

"You would be surprised at how much they have in common, Keelin."

She told her sister what she had seen when touching the pocket watch.

"Ask him about it."

"I can't."

"You can. Ask."

"I did ask before the vision. I got nothing, Keelin. I don't want to let him know that I saw his past. I want him to trust me enough to tell me. But he doesn't."

"Trust goes two ways, my darling sister. We all have wounds we try to hide. See if you can't start the healing."

Keelin knew when to give up. She changed the subject before Flanna could dig her heels in deeper.

"How are our American cousins?"

"The ones we can place—good."

"What do you mean?"

"Quinlan Farrell is missing."

"Isn't he the one who takes off mysteriously and then shows up when it suits him?"

Or so she had heard. She'd never meet her Aunt Rose's children. That branch of the family lived in someplace called South Dakota.

"Kathleen and Neil are really worried about their brother this time," Keelin said. "Apparently no one has heard from him for more than six months. Everyone is beginning to fear the worst."

Flanna sighed. The worst might be that her cousin was involved in something illicit. The fact that he was part of the McKenna Clan didn't automatically make him an honest man.

She said, "Let's hope he's found then, for Aunt Rose's sake."

Though they talked about other things for a few minutes, Keelin had an appointment to keep.

Hanging up the phone, Flanna thought about what her sister had said about Michael. Was it possible for both of them to heal and find happiness?

At the moment, her main concern was finishing the piece for the auction. She needed to get busy. First she needed to get dressed.

In the process of picking out a pair of crop pants, she heard the outside door slam open, followed by Michael bellowing, "Flanna, where are you?"

"In here."

She was just pulling up the crops when Michael stormed into the bedroom with her only half-dressed.

"Where in the hell have you been? I've been crazy with worry!"

"Making arrangements for tomorrow."

"I thought you were going to do that in town."

"Lisa suggested we go out to the golf club to get the lay of the land. And then I went in to Shannon to buy something suitable to wear tomorrow. I'm perfectly fine, Michael, as you can well see."

Suddenly he did seem to see that she was half-naked, dressed only in the unzipped crops and a demi-cup bra. He stared at her as a starving man stares at a table laden with food. Flanna flushed but refused to cover herself. The longer they stood without speaking, the more heat flowed through her, making her want something she couldn't have.

But what was wrong with having what she could, while she could?

She hesitated only a second before taking a step closer to Michael. Her pulse sped up and her mouth went dry as she said, "I do appreciate your worrying about me."

"You could have called."

"No cell, remember?"

"That's no excuse. But I'll get you one, first thing in the morning. Don't ever scare me like that again."

As if she would have the chance to do so once he was gone.

Flanna thought about telling him that her sister had called with a warning about the next day, but if she did, he might try to stop the plan. She would be all right, Flanna told herself. Security people would be all over the place, and she wouldn't wander outside alone.

Some part of her knew that might not be enough.

Some part of her knew that now might be her last opportunity to have the man she loved.

Wetting her lips, Flanna moved within a hairsbreadth of Michael and didn't miss his gaze dropping to her breasts. "I didn't mean to scare you." She flattened her hand on his chest and slowly inched it downward to his stomach. "Can I make it up to you?"

With a groan, he pulled her to him, trapping her hand between them. He kissed her lips, her neck, her breasts. Especially her breasts.

Flanna arched backward to give him full access. His tongue lathed the soft flesh, then slipped beneath the lace edge and coaxed a nipple from its hiding place. He suckled and bit it until it was hard and aching. And then he started over with the other breast.

Boneless with desire, she let him drop her back onto her bed. His mouth followed her exposed flesh downward, into the crevice left by the open zipper. Moaning, she lifted her hips to give him better access. He peeled down her crops and her lace panties inch-by-inch. And inch-by-inch he followed with his tongue until it parted her and explored deep inside her wet flesh.

Catching her fingers in his hair, Flanna pushed herself harder into his mouth until a pulsing started deep inside. His fingers sliding through her wetness made her world shatter in an instant.

Only then did he undress himself. He never took his eyes off her.

She finished undressing herself and slid up higher on the bed, opening her arms in invitation. The moment he entered her, she was ready to come again. He rocked her smooth and slow until the need was excruciating, but he wouldn't take her to completion. Taking matters into her own hands, Flanna touched herself, running her fingers between herself and him, covering them both with thick, creamy juices. She came in waves, deep and fierce, and yet he somehow held on.

Panting, she pushed him off her, then slid down so she could taste him, let him slide in and out of her mouth the way he had between her thighs. He was trying to hold back still, but unwilling to let him, she took him in so far that he couldn't escape her, not even when she felt the tremors begin. She kept him prisoner, took all he had to offer, and when he finally fell over her and kissed her more deeply than she'd ever been kissed, she held on to him as if she would never let him go.

An innocent lie. One she needed to believe at least for a little while.

SLOWING THE VEHICLE as it neared the McKenna woman's cottage, the driver sped up at the first glimpse of the man on guard outside. Damn! Now she had even more security.

Was the extra security meant to guard the ring…or had she really found a new piece of Caillech's jewelry?

If so, the stakes had just multiplied.

Two pieces to retrieve. Two pieces to complete the suite. Two pieces to give the possessor the might of a powerful and angry sorceress.

Getting that power and wielding it was worth any sacrifice. Time was running out. Tomorrow was Beltane, the day Caillech had burned at the stake.

Time to set a fire under anyone in the way.

Chapter Seventeen

"I want you to go over the suite with a fine-tooth comb," Michael told his security team the next morning when they arrived at Clondowney Golf and Country Club.

Flanna had given the events coordinator his name, so he was in possession of the keys to the suite. His men quickly made sure there were no hidden cameras, weapons, whatever. Then they set up cameras of their own and made one of the bedrooms control central and off-limits to the guests.

"Club maintenance is here, boss," one of the men told him as two uniformed men entered the suite.

"I need you to move furniture in this bedroom," Michael told the workers, indicating the room closest to the parlor. "Rearrange it to clear the central area, so there's room enough to set up the display case and guests can move around it."

"We're on it."

The museum-quality display case was a pedestal mount with tempered glass and fiber-optic lighting. Prospective buyers would be able to see the piece if not touch it. Hopefully that would prevent anyone from realizing Flanna and he were perpetrating a fraud in order to trap a criminal.

Not that they were proceeding without backup. Detective Garda Murphy knew about the setup, as did Michael's contact at Interpol. Neither would be directly involved in the execution of the plan, but assuming the plan did work, both would be available to make arrests. Michael would plant a shill in the crowd—a woman who would continually up the bid, so that if the killer tried to buy the piece, he would fail. That meant the killer would have to try to steal it, and in doing so, would be caught on camera.

Flanna had come up with a feasible plan. He just hoped the killer would play in to it.

With his men hard at work, Michael took a moment to check the grounds around the annex. Only one road out—the same way they'd come in. On the other side of the building, sheer cliffs dropped to the Atlantic below. Looking down to the foaming water that crashed against massive boulders gave his stomach something of a turn.

He hadn't forgotten the fall he'd taken in the ruins.

Or the way Flanna had saved him.

Flanna… His time with her was nearly up. Despite his best intentions to leave her be, to make the break as easy as possible, he hadn't been able to resist her allure the night before. They'd made love off and on all night, nearly to daybreak, at which time she'd gotten up to finish the pendant copy.

She'd begun by doing something called pickling—soaking the silver-and-bronze Celtic knot in a mixture of water and sulphuric acid. He'd watched, fascinated by her skill, as she'd then brass-brushed it to remove the oxide, after which she'd placed it in a tumbler with steel balls and polishing soap. The final touch had been to add the fire opal.

Only then did she go back to bed, and had passed out in sheer exhaustion.

He'd left her to sleep with a cell phone on the pillow next

to her head and a man guarding the front door. He would make sure she wasn't hurt physically. He only wished he could be so certain of her heart.

As FLANNA READIED herself for the auction, she tried to put her tenuous relationship with Michael to the back of her mind. Catching a murderer took precedence over what she wanted for herself. She needed to keep her focus on the plan and off her personal life.

Still, as she slipped into her satin charmeuse dress with a scoop neckline and empire waist, she wondered if Michael's eyes would light up when he saw her. If she told him she'd chosen the deep blue dress because the color was symbolic of Druidic protection, that light in his eyes would quickly fade with his disbelief. The only jewelry she wore was a more obvious ancient symbol of protection—a silver pentacle, or five-pointed star, surrounded by a circle.

Instinct told her she would need all the protection she could get that day.

Taking the cell phone from the pillow where Michael had left it for her, she stroked it gently with her fingertips as if she was touching him. She believed in his abilities even if he didn't believe in hers, so she slipped the cell into one of her dress's deep patch pockets. She slipped the pouched ring into the other.

Two members of Michael's team escorted her to Clondowney. One of them drove, the other carried the pendant in a fancy lockbox attached to his wrist. Her nerves were on edge and not only from their plan to trap a murderer. She would see Michael soon, and no matter that she tried to put his imminent departure from Ireland out of mind, she simply couldn't.

So when they arrived at the club and Michael wasn't in the suite, nor anywhere in sight, Flanna fought a hollow feeling inside. He was undoubtedly wrapped up in some aspect of seeing to their security, but she wished he were here so they could share a private moment before potential buyers started arriving.

No sooner had she thought it when she heard a vehicle pull up in the car park next to the building. Opening the door, she saw Lisa dressed in a tailored gray suit and carrying a garment bag and a makeup case; undoubtedly she was taking Flanna up on her offer to change in the suite.

"Where can I put this and what can I do?"

"Take the bedroom down the hall off the small parlor. As to what to do, so far we have things in hand. At least until the catering staff arrives."

Lisa peeked into the bedroom where the guy with the case attached to his wrist was unlocking the cuff. Her eyebrows shot up as she looked at Flanna.

"I'll be right back," she promised. "I want first look at the piece."

But the pendant was barely seated on its velvet-lined container in the case when Flanna heard the outer door open. Thinking Michael had returned, she had trouble breathing as she whirled around to face him.

Only Michael hadn't returned, and the smile on Flanna's face quickly faded as she met Barry Rafferty's dark gaze.

"Barry...you're early. We don't open for another hour."

"You won't open at all if I have anything to say about it. I heard about this supposedly new piece of Caillech's you just happened to mysteriously find. We both know it belonged to my mother."

"You're wrong."

"It's too coincidental to be true."

"I'm telling you that Bridget never even saw this piece or knew it existed." Where was everyone? The moment she needed backup, everyone seemed to have disappeared. "I didn't know about it until a few days ago."

"Where did you get it, then? And from who?"

Flanna's pulse was rushing, but she tried to appear calm. "My client wishes to remain anonymous. I'm merely representing the piece—"

"Hogwash!" Barry said, stepping threateningly closer. "That piece rightly belongs to the Raffertys. You'd better turn it over to me right now!"

There was a darkness about him that sent a shard of fear through Flanna. "If you want the piece, you will have to bid on it like everyone else." And if he took one step closer she would certainly scream for help.

"I'll have you arrested!"

From behind him, Michael said, "And I'll have you thrown out and barred from the auction if you don't calm down."

Flanna's knees went weak with relief. Michael stood in the open doorway looking ready for a fight despite his fine dark suit and white shirt. Though she wanted to run to him, to throw herself in his arms and let him surround her with the aura of his protection, she didn't move an inch.

"You don't belong here, Eagan," Barry said. "Why don't you mind your business in America."

"At the moment my business is here. I'll ask you to leave once, and then I'll have someone help you off the property."

"I belong to this golf club! Do you?"

Michael moved out of the doorway. "This would be the exit."

Barry gave them each a surly look before turning and heading for the door, muttering, "I'll be back."

Flanna couldn't help herself. "And I'll be looking forward to your bid."

Michael shook his head. "You do like to have the final say, don't you?"

"He makes me so angry!"

"And afraid."

Flanna shuddered at Michael's acuity. "There's a darkness in the man."

"You had one of your visions about him?"

"No. And don't be plaguing me about my foolishness now."

"Maybe I don't think you're foolish."

She blinked at him. "What? When did that change?"

"I had myself convinced that your interest in the psychic was charming and inventive. I even thought the reason you knew about the horse tattoo was because you'd actually gotten a glimpse of Begley's arm before he squeezed the breath from you. That you just didn't remember actually seeing it."

"And now?"

"And now I think there must be something to this psychic business. And to your grandmother's legacy. I don't claim to embrace it all or even to understand it. But I want to and maybe I can with time."

Flanna could hardly believe what she was hearing. Michael was broadening his thinking. She was wondering if there was hope for them, after all, when the catering staff arrived with the food.

Michael stepped out of the way of a man carrying a heavy silver server. "The place is now officially up for grabs."

The look he gave her told Flanna he regretted not having a few minutes alone with her even as she regretted the same. He disappeared into one of the bedrooms—the one with the camera monitors, she was certain. About to alert Lisa, Flanna realized the other woman was already on her way to the parlor, looking stunning in a calf-length gray sheath shot with silver threads.

"Do you think people will actually come?" Flanna asked her, knowing only that Barry Rafferty would be back.

"Several people I know said they would try to make it. You realize the lure is curiosity more than anything else. Well, that and the free food."

"I kind of guessed that. Hopefully, there will be real interest from the right source."

"And who would that be?"

"The person willing to pay a small fortune for the pendant, of course."

"You do have a formal authentication of the piece by an expert, right?"

"Right," Flanna lied.

Michael had somehow gotten a fake together in case anyone wanted to look at it. Since no one would actually lose any money here—they had a woman in place who would outbid any other interested parties—their fraudulent auction would be victimless.

Less than an hour later, they opened the doors of the suite to the public.

Barry Rafferty led the charge. "Where is it?"

Flanna indicated the open bedroom doors. "The case holding the pendant is in there. And so is a guard."

Without responding, Barry whipped away from her. She watched him walk around the case and consider the pendant from every angle. Others joined him, and from the look of resentment on his face, she knew he was holding himself back from telling them all to go to hell. No doubt because he'd believed Michael's earlier threats.

How high would Barry bid? she wondered. What would he

do to get his hands on the pendant? And of course there was still the ring that was burning a hole in her pocket.

"Well, the Rafferty boys are both here."

Not expecting Michael to sneak up on her, Flanna started. "Eamon's here? Where?"

"Food."

She glanced into the dining room and saw Eamon amongst a dozen other people all loading their plates from the buffet.

"We have a small crowd, anyway." Although she recognized a few as being Michael's security people.

"Give it some time," he said. "The auction's not for another hour."

That time went by quickly. Flanna spent most of it sizing up the real interest in the pendant as more curious, well-dressed people entered the suite. Most took a quick glance into the case, while others studied the contents ad nauseam. Were they trying to decide if the pendant really had belonged to Caillech? she wondered.

Then Katie Rafferty walked in alone. She zeroed right in on the case and then stood there, staring down at the piece, standing as still as a statue. Other people came and went but Katie didn't move and Flanna wondered if the young woman wasn't mourning her mother.

With an odd feeling, she slipped out the front door and looked to the parking lot. A black Mercedes was parked nearby. It looked like the one she'd seen in Ballyloy. Then she remembered seeing Katie getting into a Mercedes at the manor. And a dark car had tried to force them off the road.

It couldn't be…Flanna shook her head, told herself it wasn't, but the uneasy feeling followed her back inside.

Lisa said, "There you are. Your auction is going to be a big success."

"I'm counting on it." If this didn't work to nail the killer, Flanna was out of ideas. Pushing the black Mercedes from her mind, she said, "I wonder how many people will actually make a bid."

"Count me in," Lisa said. "It's a beautiful piece. I would love to own it. Wouldn't it look fabulous with this dress?"

Is that why she had worn it? Flanna wondered. "Perfect. But should you get it, you're not really going to wear it, are you? I thought you believed in the curse."

"I do. Of course. I was just daydreaming."

Suddenly Flanna spotted the Raffertys' houseman at the buffet. "What's Hugh Nolan doing here?"

Lisa shrugged. "I believe he drove Katie Rafferty here. A man's got to eat. You don't really mind that he came inside, do you?"

"No, of course not. I was just surprised."

She was also surprised that Lisa spoke of the houseman so congenially after their argument the day before. Though tempted to ask about it, Flanna held back. It would be admitting she'd seen the argument without mentioning it. An awkward situation.

Michael joined them. "It's almost time. Five minutes."

Suddenly Flanna felt as if she couldn't breathe. "I think I'll go freshen up."

"Hurry."

Nodding, she raced down the hall. Entering the bedroom where she'd left her bag, she first ran cool water over her wrists and hands, then patted her face, making her feel better. It didn't completely alleviate her nerves, but it calmed her down a bit.

She ran a brush through her loose hair and swiped a fresh coat of gloss over her lips and she was ready.

Almost.

From her pocket, she fetched the pouch and removed Caillech's ring. "Why haven't you helped me?" she murmured.

Looking deep into the fire opal, she swore she saw movement. But it was not the whirling skirts of a flamenco dancer, the only vision she had so far associated with the ring.

Instead, she saw an agitated swirl of color.

Because this was Beltane, nearing the time Caillech had died, and the sorceress was agitated?

Perhaps she *was* too imaginative, Flanna thought, a giggle bubbling up inside her. Then, remembering the things she'd seen in the cabochons while holding the various originals of the collection, she sobered.

"Caillech, are you really in there?"

The fire in the cabochon seemed to burn brighter. Her head went light and her breathing grew shallow, sensations that usually accompanied her visions. Only there was no vision, just this weird sensation that the sorceress was trying to tell her something. A psychic link of some sort.

Flanna focused more intently, determined to force the stone to give up something more substantial. Suddenly a beautiful woman with long, wild mahogany hair appeared in her mind. She wore the complete Celtic suite over a plain cerise gown. Then the vision turned to flames and the woman was screaming, being burned alive at the stake.

The vision abruptly ended, but not the sensation of the ring trying to connect with her. Trying to lead her somewhere. She opened the bedroom door, and from a distance heard the auctioneer begin.

"Who will start the bidding? Twenty-five thousand euros. Do I hear twenty-five?"

Flanna turned toward the parlor and the sensation from the ring diminished, so she turned in the other direction and the urge to go that way became intense. The ring took her straight to the last bedroom down the hall. The one Lisa had used.

She knocked but of course there was no answer. Lisa was at the auction.

Where *she* should be, Flanna thought.

Instead she went inside and the psychic prodding grew stronger, and even more intent as she approached the dressing table and the case that lay on it. Hesitating only a moment, Flanna dropped the ring back into her pocket and tentatively touched the case.

An immediate jolt akin to electricity zapped through her. Heart hammering, unable to resist, she opened the lid and looked down into a panoply of pots and tubes and brushes. Makeup. Exactly what was supposed to be there.

Then why the psychic voltage?

Starting to close the lid, Flanna realized the inside didn't go very deep—at least not as deep as the bottom of the case. The makeup-filled tray lifted off easily.

Her breath caught in her throat as she stared down at Caillech's treasures. Michael… She had to tell him. Still a bit off-kilter, she slipped the cell phone from her pocket, but barely had time to punch his number before realizing she wasn't alone.

"Find what you were looking for?"

Flanna turned her gaze from the cache of silver-and-bronze jewelry to Lisa, who was standing in the doorway. Hoping the call would go through, she dropped the still-open cell to the carpet. The auctioneer's voice echoed down the hallway behind Lisa. The bid was now up to fifty-five thousand euros.

"I believe I have found it all." Flanna lifted the intricate girdle belt out of the case. "This is what started Michael on his journey. It belonged to a woman in Boston who died tragically young."

Lisa stepped into the room and closed the door behind her. "A tiresome girl who didn't even contemplate the value of what her father gave her."

Wanting Lisa to admit she was a murderer, Flanna asked, "You had to kill her for it?"

Crossing the room toward Flanna, Lisa shrugged and avoided a direct confession. "There's always a price to pay for magic." She grabbed the girdle from Flanna's hand and put it around her own waist.

"But the legitimate owners are the ones who paid with their lives."

"Felled by the curse." Lisa dug into the case and brought out bracelets, which she slid onto her wrists.

"What about you?" Flanna said as Lisa attached the brooch to her bodice, then hung the original pendant around her neck, the chain framing the pin. "Aren't you worried you'll be next?"

Lisa laughed and put on the earrings. "It's Beltane. Rather than the wrath of Caillech, I'll get the gift of her magic."

"Only if you have the whole suite."

"But I do now."

"You don't have the second pendant."

"That fake?" Lisa laughed and secured the headpiece so the cabochon dangled in the middle of her forehead. "You can fool some people, but I'm not some people. I've studied the collection and planned how to get it for years. I knew what you were doing the moment you came up with that ridiculous story."

As she spoke, the door opened, and Michael stepped inside the bedroom. "It's over, Miss Madden. You're done."

"I think not, Mr. Eagan. I won't be done until I harness Caillech's power."

He took a good look at her and said, "You don't have the ring."

"But our dear Flanna does." Lisa grabbed Flanna's wrist with an iron grip that seemed impossible to break. "Give me the ring."

"Go to hell."

Lisa laughed. "Perhaps Caillech will take us both there."

"Let go of her," Michael ordered.

"Or you'll what?" Lisa shifted her gaze to the door. "Take care of him, darling."

Hugh Nolan stepped inside, leading with a gun.

Chapter Eighteen

Spotting Nolan in the mirror, Michael didn't give the Raffertys' houseman the chance to shoot anyone. Even as Lisa spoke, he whirled, tightened his hand and chopped across Nolan's forearm. The gun flew from the man's fingers and spun across the floor to land at Lisa's feet.

Nolan jumped him and Michael couldn't stop himself from falling back on the bed. He saw Lisa retrieve the gun just before Nolan's fist connected with his jaw, jerking his head in the other direction.

He heard the outside door open and heard the Madden woman say, "You'll be coming with me, Flanna McKenna, or I shall kill you where you stand."

Rolling off the bed, Michael used his shoulder to ram Nolan. The man stood fast like a brick wall. Worse, he rammed back with an elbow, sending Michael reeling. Though he figured Lisa was forcing Flanna out the door on the cliff side, he was too busy trying to anticipate Nolan's next move to see exactly what was happening between the women.

"Surely we can work out something…." Flanna's voice faded.

Nolan was stronger and tougher than he appeared to be, and Michael suspected he hadn't always lived to serve. The man fought dirty, like a guy off the streets, something Michael himself recognized and so was able to circumvent being badly hurt.

The longer the two women were alone, the more likely it would be for Flanna to be hurt, most probably killed. The thought nearly strangled him.

He wasn't going to let that happen.

Gathering every ounce of strength he had, Michael distracted Nolan by grabbing his throat with his left hand and squeezing hard, while making a fist with his right. The moment Nolan focused on removing the choke-hold, Michael swung and then let go of the other man's neck. Nolan popped backward slightly, and Michael connected a hard-hitting hammer fist to the side of his head.

Stunned, Nolan dropped to his knees and Michael kicked him in the gut to make sure the breath was knocked the hell out of him long enough to get assistance.

Finding his cell, he called one of the security guards while keeping an eye on Nolan to make sure the guy stayed down. "The rear bedroom, *now!* I have one of the bastards and need to go after the other."

Michael was thankful that Flanna had the presence of mind to use the cell he'd left for her on her pillow that morning. She'd kept the connection open so he'd heard her and Lisa talking, the reason he'd come running to find her.

His man came rushing into the room, said "I have him," and Michael raced out toward the cliffs, hoping he wasn't too late to save Flanna.

"WHAT DID YOU DO to bribe Hugh Nolan into going along with your plan?" Flanna asked as Lisa dragged her toward the cliff.

The crash of wave against rock sent a prickly feeling up

her spine. That and remembering her sister's phone call. Keelin had warned her....

"Bribe?" Lisa said. "Hugh *is* my plan. We've worked together to get the whole collection, though I must admit that he's a bit faint-hearted when faced with more difficult, if necessary, parts of the plan. People are really so fragile. It doesn't take much to snuff out a life."

"How did you get him to agree to help you?"

"I'm the one who recommended Hugh to Bridget when her old butler happened to disappear without warning months ago."

Hugh had already been working for Bridget when the woman had hired Flanna. Undoubtedly the old butler hadn't disappeared; he'd been buried.

Lisa went on. "Too bad Bridget had to leave Katie's place and return to the manor when she did. I really did love the woman. To think she could be alive today."

Flanna wasn't fooled by her mournful tone this time. Obviously Lisa Madden would do whatever to whomever to get what she wanted. She was a cold-hearted, cold-blooded killer.

"What does Hugh get out of the deal?" Flanna asked.

Lisa smiled a tight, ironic smile. "He's been getting *me,* darling. Any way he wants me. And when I have Caillech's powers, he'll have whatever I choose to give him. All depends on how much he continues to please me. Now *you* give *me* the ring."

"I don't think so."

Flanna knew the moment she did so, she would seal her own fate. As would Lisa. Did the woman mistakenly think she would gain the sorceress's powers without consequence? Her body might be alive, but if her spirit didn't actually die, her mind would be prisoner, controlled by Caillech.

"I think you will give me the ring," Lisa said, pulling Flanna closer to the edge so the dizzying view made her stomach turn. "Nervous? You should be. If you don't hand over the ring right now, I'll throw you off this cliff and you can see if you can fly."

Dear Lord, let there be a good ending to Keelin's dream, Flanna prayed. "I can't give you the ring. I don't have it with me."

"Liar!" Lisa swung her gun hand and the steel barrel connected with the side of Flanna's head.

Her sight went all wonky, and she had trouble staying on her feet. Suddenly she felt Lisa's hands on her and she panicked, thinking the killer was going to add another body to her mounting total. Instead, Lisa shoved her to the rocky ground and searched her. Stunned as she was, Flanna fought, but trying to stop Lisa from prodding and poking was like trying to stop a hurricane, gale force and vicious.

When Flanna heard her pocket rip, she knew Lisa had found the ring. Indeed, her expression triumphant, the other woman held it out to look into the cabochon.

"This is it, then. The moment I've been waiting for."

"Don't do it," Flanna warned her, getting into a sitting position. Her head felt a little light, but she carefully got back to her feet. She had to stop Lisa. "You'll be no match for such a powerful sorceress. She's killed many times over her treasures."

"That makes two of us."

"What makes you think you'll be any different from her other victims?"

Flanna had visions—nightmares—of a powerful and vicious sorceress melding with a determined and vicious killer. God knew what disaster might ensue from such a marriage.

"I'm alive." Laughing, Lisa slipped the ring on her finger

and admired it some more. "Come, Caillech, fulfill the prophecy and cede your powers to me."

But just as Flanna feared, the sorceress would cede nothing without a struggle. Lisa began to shake and her expression changed in an instant. Her eyes grew wide, her mouth formed an *O*, her nostrils flared and her body started to jerk as if something was trying to climb inside.

"She's trying to kill me!" Lisa shrilled.

Flanna could see Caillech fighting to live again. She could see the shadow of the sorceress, masses of mahogany hair around a pale face, fluttering around a bloodred gown. It was the same image she'd seen earlier. Lisa fought back, two killers vying for dominance of one body.

Lisa screamed, the sound agonized. Her flesh was rippling, looked about to burst open.

"Take off the ring!" Flanna shouted. "It's your only hope! Break up the suite!"

Lisa tried to put her hands together to do so, but they wouldn't meet. "I can't." Expression stricken, she looked to Flanna. "I don't want to disappear forever. Help me, please. I'll reward you well!"

The only reward Flanna wanted was to see the deaths stop and for Lisa and Hugh to pay for what they'd done. Grabbing Lisa's hand, she got hold of the ring and even though the other woman struggled against her—rather, the spirit of Caillech did—she managed to dislodge it.

With Lisa still thrashing and the ring falling to the ground, Flanna ducked and got herself away from the treacherous drop. As she backed up a few steps, so did Lisa, right to the cliff's very edge.

Her expression panicked, Lisa looked down and though she

screamed and fought to keep her balance, in the end she lost the battle. Then it was she who was flailing, her body out of control as she tried to fly.

Failing, Lisa Madden lunged headfirst toward the greedy sea-foamed rocks below.

Flanna could only stand there, immobilized, until Michael's hands on her shoulders turned her around, straight into his protective arms. "It's all right," he whispered to her. "Everything is all right now."

FLANNA AWOKE feeling empty and lost after a mostly sleepless night. Michael had been there at her side to hold her and comfort her through most of it.

"It wasn't your fault," he'd said over and over. "Lisa's desire for power is what killed her."

She knew that. She did. But every time she drifted off, her subconscious replayed the scene on the cliff.

Was there something she could have said, something she could have done to stop Lisa?

It seemed to her there should have been.

She'd wanted the deaths to stop, and now Lisa made one more victim. And then there were Caillech's treasures, all rescued from the sea along with Lisa's body.

The curse still lived.

The clock told her the morning was half-gone. As was Michael, who was nowhere in the cottage, though one of his men stood outside the front door.

Flanna washed and dressed and, the thought of food knotting her stomach, made herself a cuppa, using a calming recipe Gran had taught her.

Even the tea didn't want to go down. Her throat felt closed, her chest tight, her stomach knotted.

This was the end then. Goodbye.

Where was Michael? Surely she would see him before he left for Boston. Surely he wouldn't leave without kissing her one last time, giving her one more memory she could treasure more than any tangible thing.

His imminent loss made her think of Gran's legacy. A legacy that would be lost to her forever now. He had her heart and she would never give it to another.

When she heard a car drive up, she ran to the door and saw the Renault. It was Michael.

She backed off and waited before the door, her heart pounding, every inch of her quaking with her imminent loss.

The moment he came in, looking grand in his dark suit and white shirt, he cupped her shoulders with gentle hands. "You're looking better. Good."

She wanted to ask why he didn't just take her in his arms and kiss her.

Instead, she said, "I missed you."

"You were sleeping when I left and I didn't want to wake you. I went to see Barry Rafferty." Letting go of her, he pulled a rectangular piece of paper from his breast pocket. "First, here's what he owes you."

She stared at the cashier's check in his hand, not knowing if she should touch it.

"You earned it. You didn't cause any of this grief. You helped stop it."

"Only temporarily. Who knows what the Raffertys will do with Caillech's jewelry?"

"I know." He forced the check into her hand and she set it

on a shelf. "They're going to donate it to the Irish Museum as their mother wanted."

"They agreed?"

He nodded. "Apparently young Katie forced them to do it. Samuel Holmes and Ned Easton agreed, as well. Their pieces won't go to the Irish Museum but to the British and Boston museums. The entire collection will be locked up forever but not together, so Caillech can never have another shot at regaining her mortality."

"You say that as if you never doubted Caillech would try to come back."

"I do. I may be a slow starter in this area, but I've come to believe in curses and legacies. And in fairies. Most of all, I believe in you, Flanna McKenna."

Her heart thumped unevenly. He'd told her the day before that his beliefs had broadened, but...

"Are you saying you believe in the McKenna Legacy?"

"I do, but—"

"What?"

"I haven't been totally honest with you, Flanna. I've wanted to tell you but I was afraid of losing what I had." He pulled the watch with the cracked face from his pocket. "It happened a long time ago."

"Your da and brother being gunned down," she said softly, remembering the horrible vision. "After the attack at the ruins, when you showered in the trailer, I was putting your things in order and...I saw it happen."

"You didn't say anything."

"I'm ashamed to admit that first I thought terrible things about you. And then I realized I was mistaken. I know who you are, Michael Eagan, and you're no criminal."

"But I am. Was. Or at least I was on my way to being one. I was only in high school when I begged Dad to let me become part of his operation. I was pretty smart and he wanted me to go to college, to make something of myself, he said. I wanted him to love me like he did my brother and I thought I had to be like him."

"Of course he loved you. He wanted more for you than he was able to have for himself. Perhaps your brother wasn't capable of doing that for himself."

"I understand that now. Then I simply thought Dad was trying to shove me away from him. I did small jobs for the business. Delivered messages, mostly. Ran numbers for them."

"Numbers?"

"Illegal gambling. Then I stood guard during this robbery my brother masterminded. When he found out, Dad nearly skinned us both alive and forbade me from having anything to do with his business. After high school, Dad and I fought about my going to college all summer. I wanted to talk to him about it, to tell him I made up my mind I wasn't going to do it, that I wanted to work for him and that was it. I went looking for him at the wrong time."

"The day he and your bother were killed?"

"And my uncle. I saw the whole thing. I recognized the guy who killed them, Flanna—an enforcer from a rival Irish gang—and I couldn't do anything about it. My word wasn't good enough and there was no evidence. I was determined to get proof. I went to a friend of Dad's from the old neighborhood—a private investigator who took me under his wing. He promised me that if I went to college like Dad wanted, he would teach me how to get enough proof to nail the bastard."

"And you did?"

He shook his head. "I went to school and learned the P.I. business. But in the meantime, the man who murdered my family took a bullet in the spine, became a quadriplegic. The D.A. said with that kind of injury, he would never serve time. There was no point in wasting the taxpayers' money in going through with a trial. Beside, he was no longer a threat to anyone."

"That's terrible. You must have been heartbroken."

Michael nodded. "That failure stayed with me, Flanna, that feeling of being powerless to get justice for my own. Sure, my dad and uncle and brother were criminals, too, but they were petty criminals. They never killed anyone, never even hurt anyone that I know of. So I took a stand and decided that where I could, I would make a difference to someone else. That's why I had to come to Ireland. That's why I fell in love with you. You had that same sense of responsibility to Lisa's victims."

"Why couldn't you tell me this before?"

"After we were together in the ruins, when you told me about Erin Cassidy and how you never would have been with him if you had known about his crimes…"

"You thought I would feel the same about you."

"Do you? I'll understand if you want me to leave. I get it, I really do."

He didn't want to leave, then! He wanted to stay. Joy filled Flanna.

"You get me, Michael Eagan," she told him, a smile on her lips. "If you want me. You were a boy trying to emulate your da and your brother, is all. You didn't understand what they were doing was wrong."

"No, I did know what they were doing was wrong. I just wasn't clear enough on the consequences. Or on how it affected their victims."

"But you changed and lived the life your da wanted for you. You took a route that brought you to me. You're a good and just man, Michael Eagan, and 'tis love I have for you. You are my grandmother's legacy to me."

Michael didn't argue, simply swept her into his arms, kissed her breathless and held her tight, as if he would never let her go. They might be from different worlds, different countries, but Flanna knew they would work it out and be together forever.

* * * * *

Stay tuned for the last
McKENNA LEGACY—Quin's story

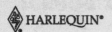

REQUEST YOUR FREE BOOKS!

2 FREE NOVELS PLUS 2 FREE GIFTS!

HARLEQUIN®

INTRIGUE®

Breathtaking Romantic Suspense

HI08

HARLEQUIN
More Than Words

"I have never felt more needed as a physician…"

—**Dr. Ricki Robinson,** real-life heroine

*Dr. Ricki Robinson is a Harlequin More Than Words
award winner and an **Autism Speaks** volunteer.*

SUPPORTING CAUSES OF CONCERN TO WOMEN

HARLEQUIN

WWW.HARLEQUINMORETHANWORDS.COM

MTW07ROB1

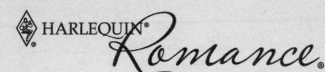

HARLEQUIN *Romance*

presents

Planning perfect weddings...
finding happy endings!

Amidst the rustle of satins and silks, the scent of red roses
and white lilies and the excited chatter of brides-to-be, six
friends from Boston are The Wedding Belles—they make
other people's wedding dreams come true....

But are they always the wedding planner...never the bride?

Who will be the next to say "I do"?

In April: Shirley Jump, *Sweetheart Lost and Found*
In May: Myrna Mackenzie, *The Heir's Convenient Wife*
In June: Melissa McClone, *S.O.S. Marry Me*
In July: Linda Goodnight, *Winning the Single Mom's Heart*
In August: Susan Meier, *Millionaire Dad, Nanny Needed!*
In September: Melissa James, *The Bridegroom's Secret*

*And don't miss the exciting wedding-planner tips and
author reminiscences that accompany each book!*

www.eHarlequin.com   HRI7507

the DEVIL'S footprints

Don't miss
the latest thriller from

AMANDA STEVENS

On sale March 2008!

- -

SAVE $1.00 off the purchase price of THE DEVIL'S FOOTPRINTS by Amanda Stevens.

Offer valid from March 1, 2008 to May 31, 2008. Redeemable at
participating retail outlets. Limit one coupon per purchase.

52608155

5 65373 00076 2   (8100) 0 11460

MAS2530CPN

SPECIAL EDITION™

Introducing a brand-new miniseries

Men of Mercy Medical

Gabe Thorne moved to Las Vegas to open a
new branch of his booming construction
business—and escape from a recent tragedy.
But when his teenage sister showed up pregnant
on his doorstep, he really had his hands full.
Luckily, in turning to Dr. Rebecca Hamilton for
the medical care his sister needed, he found
a cure for himself....

Starting with

THE MILLIONAIRE
AND THE M.D.

by *TERESA SOUTHWICK,*

available in April wherever books are sold.

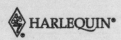

INTRIGUE®

COMING NEXT MONTH

#1053 MATCHMAKING WITH A MISSION by B.J. Daniels
Whitehorse, Montana
No matter how much Nate Dempsey's past haunted him,
McKenna Bailey couldn't keep him off her mind. He'd returned to town
to bury his troubled youth—but she wouldn't stop pursuing him until
he was working the ranch by her side.

#1054 POSITIVE I.D. by Kathleen Long
The Body Hunters
In order to save his family from ruthless killers, Will Connor made the
ultimate sacrifice. Dying. Now facing the greatest challenge of his life,
Will must come out of hiding to rescue his captive wife, Maggie, and
protect his family when they need him the most.

#1055 72 HOURS by Dana Marton
Thriller
Parker McCall never stopped loving Kate Hamilton. So when rebels
attack the Russian embassy and take his ex-wife hostage, Parker gets
to prove it. Unsanctioned and nearly impossible, this mission's nothing
without showing Kate the man—the secret agent—he really is.

#1056 SILENT WITNESS by Leona Karr
With a killer hunting for the witness to his terrible crime, an entire
town was at stake. Detective Ryan Darnell had more than one life
to save—yet teacher Marian Richards may be the most valuable of
them all.

#1057 I'LL BE WATCHING YOU by Tracy Montoya
Adriana Torres was headed for heartbreak, and Detective Daniel Cardenas
was the last person she needed on her protection detail. Worse, Daniel
wouldn't let Adriana out of his sight—but neither would a killer who
everyone thought was dead.

#1058 LOVING THE ENEMY by Pat White
Kyle McKendrick vowed to protect Andrea Franks at all costs from the
rogue military faction hunting her. But Kyle was a mercenary, and the one
man she could never forgive. Even if everything she knew about him was
wrong.

www.eHarlequin.com

HICNM0308